"Are you sure you'

The skin on Violet's arr
sat up. He couldn't help
her chest beneath her shirt.

Oblivious to the sexy direction of his thoughts, she scoffed playfully. "You mean aside from my wounded pride?"

He grinned at her and sank down on the bed. He still felt the drumbeat of arousal. Winking, he teased back, "I kind of like you as a damsel in distress."

She crossed her arms over her breasts. "You're so funny."

He shifted closer. "I'm serious, Violet."

Her heart raced. She didn't know whether it was the fact they were suddenly both in the oddly unexpected situation that had them responsible for the future of baby Ava, or the fact that he was—and always had been—so damn sexy.

Dear Reader,

We all have our notions of what makes the perfect date, relationship or even life. We all also have a practical side that tells us while everything is not absolutely fabulous all the time, it's still more than enough to make us happy.

Triplet Violet McCabe is a single physician, looking for a big change in her life. She's not happy unless everything is as perfect as it can be. Gavin Monroe is also a single physician and Violet's friend. He's not looking for any major change in his life. He figures his world is fine, just as it is.

Enter orphaned newborn baby Ava. Ava is relying on her temporary guardians, Violet and Gavin, to get her through a tough start to life and find her a great forever home and family.

Gavin and Violet take their responsibility seriously. They don't expect to fall in love with each other, and with the baby in their care, in the process. But they do, and that leads to an even bigger dilemma. Are they the right parents for Ava? Are they the right mates for each other? Both agree nothing is perfect in their temporary home and family. The question is, should it be...?

I hope you enjoy the fifth book in the McCabe Multiples series. For this and information on other titles, please visit me on Facebook or at cathygillenthacker.com.

Happy reading!

Cathy Gillen Thacker

LONE STAR BABY

Cathy Gillen Thacker

HARLEQUIN® AMERICAN ROMANCE®

Recycling programs
for this product may
not exist in your area.

ISBN-13: 978-0-373-75582-0

Lone Star Baby

Copyright © 2015 by Cathy Gillen Thacker

✦ HARLEQUIN®

™ www.Harlequin.com

Printed in U.S.A.

Cathy Gillen Thacker is married and a mother of three. She and her husband spent eighteen years in Texas and now reside in North Carolina. Her mysteries, romantic comedies and heartwarming family stories have made numerous appearances on bestseller lists, but her best reward, she says, is knowing one of her books made someone's day a little brighter. A popular Harlequin author for many years, she loves telling passionate stories with happy endings, and thinks nothing beats a good romance and a hot cup of tea! You can visit Cathy's website, cathygillenthacker.com, for more information on her upcoming and previously published books, recipes and a list of her favorite things.

Books by Cathy Gillen Thacker

Harlequin American Romance

McCabe Multiples

Runaway Lone Star Bride
Lone Star Christmas
Lone Star Valentine
Lone Star Daddy

McCabe Homecoming

The Texas Lawman's Woman
The Long, Hot Texas Summer
The Texas Christmas Gift
The Texas Wildcatter's Baby

Legends of Laramie County

The Reluctant Texas Rancher
The Texas Rancher's Vow
The Texas Rancher's Marriage
The Texas Rancher's Family

Visit cathygillenthacker.com for more titles.

Chapter One

"So it's true? You're really going to do this?"

Violet McCabe swung toward the sound of the low, gravelly voice. Gavin Monroe stood framed in the open doorway of the partially converted stable-house, dark brows lowered over his mesmerizing blue eyes.

"Do what?" she parried back, trying not to be swayed by the determination radiating from his tall, masculine frame or the sensual curve of his lips. "Go glamping for the next three months?" She was baiting her ruggedly confident colleague. "Or say no to the attending-physician position at Laramie Community Hospital?" One of two positions that had been offered to her.

Gavin strode closer, all indomitable male. "Both."

Pulse jumping, she watched as his gaze swept the exposed wooden beams supporting the high pitched roof and the large ceiling fan whirring overhead. Then it moved downward to take in the autumn sunlight pouring in through the windows of the rustic, cement-floored space she was about to call home.

"Glamping is going to be fun." She pointed to the Conestoga wagon that would serve as her bedroom. The area in front, which held a couple of braided wool rugs and her living and dining room furniture, would comprise her entertaining space. To one side of that was a hallway that led to a small utilitarian bathroom with shower, sink and commode.

On the other side of the sliding, front barn doors was her camp kitchen.

"You think so now." He walked closer to the metal sink, antique wooden worktable and shelving unit. "But when you tire of such a primitive setup…"

When it came to cooking for one, Violet knew there was little she couldn't do here. Except maybe entertain her parents, five sisters and four brothers-in-law and all their kids.

She shrugged and stepped close enough to inhale the crisp male scent of his cologne. "Then I'll go into town or visit friends and family." She had plenty living in the area.

He folded his arms across his brawny chest. "We need you at the hospital."

And she needed a new lease on life, more desperately than anyone knew.

Feeling simultaneously flattered and annoyed, Violet swallowed. "Gavin, we've been over this." More than once, as it happens, over the past year. With the same result.

He nodded tersely. "You've talked. I've listened."

And never once believed she was serious, she thought with a beleaguered sigh. "You know why I can't stay on at LCH." There was too much scrutiny here, too many people wondering if she would ever get past her grief over her late fiancé or be able to move on the way they wished. Too many people hell-bent on helping her do just that. Including and especially Gavin.

He called on the rapport they'd built as casual friends and coworkers. "What I know is that you're making a mistake."

This had a familiar ring. Her parents had said the same thing. Only her five sisters seemed to understand her need to reset the clock and strike out on her own again. "It's mine to make," she said just as stubbornly. "I need a fresh start, Gavin."

Tension filled the silence between them.

His lips thinned. "This is about Sterling, then."

And the secret unrequited lust I feel for you.

"The point is, I'm in a rut." Violet ignored the mention of the only man she had ever loved and the painful reminder of the many ways she had let him down, despite her intentions otherwise.

The way she had begun to fear she might someday let her patients down, too.

Resolutely, Violet continued. "And now, given that my residency has officially ended—"

"You still have staff privileges for another few weeks," Gavin reminded her, clearly holding out hope.

"Until the new attending, Tara Warren, comes in to take over." Violet stalked out to the U-Haul trailer that held the rest of her things. Aware he was hot on her heels, she pointed out, "Which will be by the first of October, I'm told. Until then, I'll help out, on an as-needed basis, as promised, while simultaneously honoring my commitment to my family to oversee the renovation of the new McCabe House."

Lifting a heavy box into her arms, she nodded at the rambling Victorian farmhouse on the other side of the lawn. Home of her late grandparents, John and Lilah McCabe, the two-hundred-and-fifty-acre property was being turned into a hospitality center and temporary lodging for patients and families undergoing medical crises.

"How's that going?" Wordlessly, Gavin stepped up to give her a hand, his shoulder bumping hers in the process.

Tingling where their bodies had collided, as well as everywhere they had not, Violet wheeled the loaded dolly into the stable-house. He walked beside her, easily carrying what she could only wheel. "They're supposed to start the remodeling process next week."

She emptied the dolly and returned for another load, Gavin still at her side. "How many suites are there going to be?" he asked.

After unloading, Violet paused to show him the building plans, which were spread out over her desk. "Seven—all with private baths." She flipped through the plans, pointing as she spoke. "The entire downstairs will sport a large kitchen and one living and dining area."

"It was pretty great what your grandparents did."

Violet nodded. "And fitting, in a way, for them to deed their entire estate to the formation of a nonprofit foundation dedicated to providing food and shelter for families undergoing medical crises. Given that the two of them were the driving forces that established Laramie Community Hospital in the first place, more than seventy years ago."

"I admire what they've done. What you've volunteered to do. But you don't have to live out here for three months to watch the workers, Violet." His stormy blue eyes drifted over her. "You could easily supervise this process from town, too. And still take the part-time staff physician position in the oncology department, until it becomes full-time sometime late next year. Or stay on part-time, if you want, and let them hire another part-time doc, too."

Violet knew there were a lot of options available to her, should she decide she wanted to stay on at LCH. The chief of the department had made it clear they would work with her on that score.

But being around the hospital meant being around Gavin. A lot. And that was a problem for her, because despite the soul-crushing blows life had dealt her, she still wanted desperately to believe that a fairy-tale life was possible.

Whereas Gavin, who had also weathered some devastating life events, believed their experiences proved that no such utopia existed—or ever would.

Leery of having his cynicism engender even more doubts, she'd elected to create a healthy distance between herself and her gifted colleague.

Hopeful that her alone time would bring back her inherent optimism, she said, "I want to be here, Gavin." Aware he wouldn't let it go, she said, "I need to take a break. And it's got to be a big one."

IT WASN'T THE first time Gavin Monroe had heard the sentiment. His ex-fiancée had said pretty much the same thing before walking out the door four years earlier. And while he hadn't minded so much then, he found he minded a lot now. Maybe because he was closer to Violet than any other woman who had come into his life.

Which was strange. Because they hadn't dated. Or acted on the simmering physical attraction between them in any way.

Not because he hadn't wanted to, but because he had known Violet was still carrying a torch for her own first love.

He had respected that for a time.

Envied it, really, because he had never felt the kind of all-encompassing love and passion for anyone that Violet had apparently felt for Sterling.

But now, well, the ghost in their lives was beginning to get a little old. It was time Violet moved on and became romantically involved with someone else. Unfortunately, it wouldn't be him if she wasn't here. Which was yet another reason why he had to convince the lovely physician to stay.

"At least give up on the glam camping. Move back into town." Violet paused to take an elastic hair band off her wrist. Lifting her long, chocolate-brown hair off her neck, she twisted the thick, silky strands into a knot on top of her head. The casual updo brought even more attention to the classically beautiful features of her oval face. "I already gave up my place."

He inhaled the fragrance of her perfume and felt his heartbeat quicken. "So stay with me."

"You can't be serious."

He shrugged. "I'm only there half the time."

"You also live in a shotgun house," Violet scoffed. "With—what?—a thousand square feet of space."

"More like nine hundred. And there's nothing wrong with small houses. It has to be better than an un-air-conditioned barn."

"First of all, it's September. So the worst of the heat has passed. And with the barn doors open, the ceiling fan going, it's quite comfortable, even in the middle of the day."

Of course she wasn't uncomfortable. She had on a pair of khaki shorts that ended at midthigh and showcased her spectacular legs. A short-sleeved, V-necked T-shirt that did the same for her trim midriff and lusciously full breasts. He, on the other hand, was burning up in a pair of jeans and an open-necked knit shirt. Sizzling hot from below the waist.

"I don't understand why everyone is so skeptical about my plan to camp out here for the next couple of weeks."

Ever the idealist, he imagined she had all sorts of romantic notions—dramatized nicely by the white-organza-covered Conestoga wagon slash bedroom with the set of custom-made wooden steps leading up to it.

Trying not to think of what was inside that wagon, except a no-doubt very comfy, very femininely outfitted bed, he said, "Maybe because you're not really the outdoorsy type?"

Mischief twinkled in her eyes. "Exactly why I'm 'glamping' instead of camping."

He gave her a long, assessing glance, taking in every pampered inch of her. His desire to protect her intensified. "You got hot water in that shower back there?"

Violet opened her mouth. Shut it.

Which confirmed, Gavin thought, she didn't know.

"I'm sure it will be fine," she said stubbornly.

He couldn't help it. He laughed.

She dismissed him with an airy wave of her delicate hand. "I have some money saved. I could always put in a water heater if I want one."

He moved in close enough to goad. "Doesn't that defeat the purpose of *glamping*, having too many of the usual conveniences?"

Violet huffed, her cheeks turning an enticing pink, and stepped back from him. "I really don't see why you're so concerned with my comfort, but I really wish—" She stopped at the beeping of his cell phone.

Reluctantly, he lifted it off his belt. "Dr. Monroe."

"Hey, Gavin. It's Mitzy Martin."

Laramie County's premier social worker.

"I have to talk to you," the amiable thirtysomething went on, as direct as always. "Preferably in person. Where are you?"

He watched Violet go back to carrying in belongings. "McCabe House."

He wandered out to lend a hand. "Is Violet McCabe there by chance?" Mitzy continued.

With a smile he said, "She's standing right in front of me," and gestured for Violet to wait—that he'd carry the box of books she was contemplating.

Violet's brow furrowed.

"Great!" Mitzy enthused. "I need to see her, too. I'll be right there." She hung up before he could ask anything else.

Clipping his phone back on his belt, he reached out to relieve Violet of the box she had once again started to pick up. "Mitzy Martin wants to speak to us."

"Any idea why?"

"She didn't say." But knowing Mitzy as well as he did, it had to be something important.

"LET'S ALL SIT DOWN, shall we?"

Violet wasn't surprised that Mitzy got right down to business. Nor did she mind.

Spending too much time in close quarters with Gavin Monroe always left her feeling off-kilter. Frankly, she needed a chaperone where he was concerned, so she was *glad* for the extra company. Lest she find herself forgetting her usual reserve and acting on the innate restlessness she felt these days.

As soon as the three of them were situated comfortably around the table, Mitzy turned on her laptop computer and clicked on the appropriate file. She turned the screen so everyone could see it. "You-all remember Tammy Barlowe and her husband, Jared?"

Violet nodded. "They came into the ER last spring when Jared fell ill during a weekend trip to Lake Laramie. Gavin stabilized him. I was called in because he was a stage four cancer patient." *Having a last hurrah with his teenage wife.*

"You also know that Jared died last summer."

"Tammy wrote us, to let us know." Violet struggled to contain the lump in her throat. "It wasn't all bad news, though. She was pregnant. In fact, shouldn't she be due to deliver in a couple of weeks?"

"That's what we need to talk about," Mitzy said solemnly. "It wasn't just Jared who was sick. Tammy had a heart condition that made carrying a baby unwise. She chose to ignore medical advice and get pregnant anyway. Although Ava was born a month early, she's fine."

"And Tammy?" Gavin asked.

Mitzy shook her head. "Her heart wasn't strong enough. She died during childbirth."

Violet laid a hand over her heart. "Oh, no…"

Gavin squeezed Violet's hand.

She relaxed into his grip, accepting the quiet comfort he offered.

"Because she knew her death was a possibility, she left a videotaped will of her wishes." Her expression still solemn, Mitzy clicked on the file.

Tammy Barlowe appeared on the screen. She was clad in a hospital gown and robe. Her short brown bob looked lackluster, her freckles stood out beneath her pale skin, and there were pronounced dark circles beneath her eyes. And yet there was a serenity about her; a deep maternal happiness that seemed to shine through despite her physical difficulties. Hand protectively cupping her swollen belly, she looked straight into the camera and said, "Hey, Dr. McCabe, Dr. Monroe. If you're seeing this, it means I'm not here anymore…but my baby girl, Ava, is. And that means she needs a home and family to watch over her."

Tammy swallowed. Lower lip trembling, she pushed on. "I wish Jared and I had relatives we could call on, but we don't." She paused to look long and hard at her audience. "And the last thing either of us ever wanted was to have a child of ours grow up the way we did, in the foster care system."

A soft sound of dissent was heard in the background.

Tammy grinned and lifted a hand at her off-camera audience. "No offense to the social system that helped us, and the social workers and legal aid attorneys who are helping me now. But being a ward of the state is not the same as living with parents who love you and will make sure you grow up right." Clearing her throat, she glanced toward the camera again. "Which is where you come in, Dr. McCabe. You're not just a great lady doc, you're everything I ever wanted in a mom. And, Dr. Monroe, you're everything I ever wanted in a dad."

Violet could see that Gavin would make a wonderful father. Not that she'd ever heard him talk about wanting kids. Or *not* wanting them, either…

Tammy continued with her trademark enthusiasm. "Both of you were so wonderful to me and Jared. And you work so well together when it comes to caring for people." Another long pause. "And I also know, 'cause I did a little checking, that neither of you is married or has any other kids of your own…"

She hitched in a bolstering breath. "So I'm asking you both to step in, in the event of my demise, and adopt my Ava together. You don't have to be married or anything. Just be the mom and dad she needs."

Violet turned to Gavin, who looked as stunned as she was.

"But if you both can't do that, or if one of you wants to and the other doesn't, that's fine." Tammy sighed, as if already having anticipated being disappointed on that score. "I'm okay with just one of you becoming her actual legal guardian, as long as she has extended family—like either the Monroe or the McCabe clans—to take care of her. So that no matter what, she will never end up in the system…" Tammy teared up. "And will always have family around to raise her."

That, really, Violet thought, her heart going out to her late patient, wasn't too much to want.

More murmurs could be heard prompting in the background.

Tammy turned back to the camera. "It's a big decision. You both will need time to think about it and discuss it with each other."

Quietly, she pleaded, "While you are doing that, I'm

going to ask that you personally care for my little girl rather than put her in foster care. Until such time one of you but preferably both decide to raise Ava as your own—which is what I hope will happen—or can work with the social workers to find a suitable adoptive family. One with a lot of close relatives as backup to ensure she is loved, no matter what."

Again, Violet thought, realizing how much she counted on the extensive McCabe clan for love and support, it was not too much to ask for. Gavin had a big, loving family in the Monroe clan, too.

"Ideally, I'd also like Ava to be raised in or around Laramie, Texas, so you can watch over her and if not be her parents, at least be her godparents as she grows up. What I want most for my daughter is for her to be cherished. And I know the two of you have hearts big enough to do just that. So—" Tammy swallowed hard, moisture glistening in her eyes "—thanks. For everything you did for me and Jared last summer and everything you're going to do for my darling Ava."

Tammy wiped a tear from her cheek. A murmur could be heard in the background. She nodded and the video ended.

"I realize this is a lot to hit you with, which is why I wanted to talk to you in person," Mitzy said.

No kidding, Violet thought. Her heart had been turned inside out just hearing about the situation. And she hadn't even met the little darling yet.

Gavin had to be equally thrown by the request, yet it was impossible for her to tell from his inscrutable expression.

Still feeling a little shell-shocked, Violet swung back to Mitzy. "Where's the baby now?"

"In the hospital in Dallas, where she was born two weeks ago."

"Two weeks?" Gavin echoed at last.

"Ava came into the world only weighing four pounds."
Mitzy went on to explain the medical problems the preemie had already endured, which included breathing strug-
gles, weight loss, feeding issues and difficulty absorbing
nutrients.

"She won't be released until she's into a regular bassinet, taking food from a bottle and gaining the appropriate
weight. But if you two are willing to become legal guardians, at least temporarily, we could transport her by the
end of the week to the hospital here. Naturally, it helps that
you're both physicians."

And hence would be better equipped to help a struggling newborn, Violet thought, switching quickly into
caretaker mode.

The social worker lifted her hand. "I know neither of
you had any idea you'd been named as Ava's legal guardian. Never mind consented to Tammy's request. So I don't
want—or expect—either of you to give me an answer
about any of this right now. Talk it over with each other
before making a decision."

Gavin nodded his understanding.

"We'll get back to you tomorrow," Violet promised, still
feeling a little dazed.

Mitzy gathered her belongings and left.

Gavin turned to Violet, his expression serious, intense.
"So," he said heavily, seeming to be in as much a quandary as she was, "what do we do?"

Chapter Two

The usual idealism shining in her pretty brown eyes, Violet turned to Gavin, frowned and said, "Obviously, we can't adopt baby Ava together." She walked back outside and he followed her. "We barely know each other."

Barely?

While it was true they hadn't hung out together as kids and had run in different social circles—it was certainly different now that they were both physicians.

Irked to find her so quick to discount the time they *had* spent together, Gavin stepped in once again to lend a hand unpacking the trailer. "We've worked together for the past five years while we completed our residencies and fellowship training."

"You know what I mean. Yes, I know your preferred ways of dealing with certain medical situations, just as you surely know mine. But when it comes to the intricate personal details of your life, I don't know you any better than I know the rest of the staff at the hospital." Violet plucked a lamp base out of the pile of belongings, rooting around until she found the shade. "And you don't really know me at all, either."

Gavin's jaw tightened. Oh, he knew her, all right. Maybe better than she thought.

For instance, he knew her preferred coffee was a skinny vanilla latte. And that she loved enchiladas above all else—to the point she'd sampled all twenty-five types from the local Tex-Mex restaurant.

He tore his gaze from the barest hint of cleavage in the vee of her T-shirt and concentrated instead on the dismayed blush of color sweeping her delicate cheeks.

"And whose fault is that?" he inquired huskily.

"Mine, obviously," she said with a temperamental lift of her finely arched brow, "since I prefer to keep a firewall between my professional and private lives."

More like a nuclear shield, he thought grimly.

Having tried to pierce it once or twice himself, he'd given up and concentrated on his own work, moving on to occasionally date other women. Except for his one disastrous engagement, none of those relationships had ever amounted to anything more than a short-lived flirtation. Mostly because none of the other women had even begun to measure up to the sexy, irrepressible Violet McCabe.

He gazed into her eyes, chiding, "What private life?"

She looked down her nose at him, lamp and shade still in hand, as he stacked moving boxes onto the wheeled dolly. "You are too funny, Monroe." She stepped back reluctantly to let him push the dolly into the barn for her.

Realizing how ridiculous it was to still be lusting after her when she was still not over losing Sterling, Gavin gestured to the place she'd been putting all the other boxes.

She nodded her approval and he set them down.

"Besides," she taunted, watching as he straightened to his full six feet three inches, "it's not as if you have a viable personal life, either."

Unable to resist teasing her, he raked his eyes up and down her body. "Sure about that?"

She flushed. Hinting, to his pleasure, that she might be a little more interested in him, too, than she'd previously let on.

Violet grabbed the dolly and headed back out to the

truck, her hips swaying provocatively beneath her shorts. "Let's just say I find it highly unlikely," she shot back. "Unless you've managed to get by on zero sleep the past four years—"

So she *did* know exactly how long it had been since his engagement to Penelope had ended.

"—and, the occasional cursory date aside, skirt around without detection. Which would be an even larger feat, given what an eligible bachelor you are."

Clasping a palm to his chest, as if he had just taken an arrow to the heart, he drawled, "Women find me eligible?"

She mimed exasperation at his clowning around. "Please," she said in an unamused voice that completely belied the twinkle in her eyes. She paused to put the two parts of the lamp together. "Like they don't come into the ER and hit on you every day."

They did. But a lot of single guys on the EMT, fire and sheriff's squads came in just to flirt with her, too.

"Besides…" Bending, and giving him a very nice view of her luscious derriere, she rummaged through another box marked Fragile and emerged with a cardboard sleeve of lightbulbs. With an indignant sniff, she finished putting together the lamp. "Between your extended family and mine, and the nonstop demands of our residencies and fellowships, neither of us has had time to pursue anything remotely meaningful on our own."

Which was, Gavin thought, yet another problem that had to be addressed.

Their residencies were over now.

Yes, they were still doctors with crazy work schedules, but they also deserved more of a personal life. He intended to find one.

He hoped she would, too.

"And," she continued, brushing a hand through her sexy, side-swept bangs, "I don't know if that will ever change."

The unmistakable ache in her tone caught him unaware.

He studied her, for the first time realizing she might also be a little lonely, deep down. As well as privately longing for more, too. Despite her avowals to the contrary.

"So you're thinking that because we both have so little spare time and energy on our hands, that we should just say no to Tammy's request and hand the baby over to Dallas social services?"

"No." Violet looked at him long and hard. "I'm saying we should say *yes* to *temporary* guardianship. Bring Ava here, make sure she gets absolutely everything she needs medically and then—once we're sure she is okay—have Mitzy help us find her a loving family who will welcome us as godparents and allow us to watch over her as she grows up."

Gavin heaved a sigh of relief, glad to find her being as pragmatic, compassionate and levelheaded as the situation demanded. Having been orphaned himself, albeit when he was about to enter medical school, he couldn't live with himself if he turned his back on another parentless child.

It was bad enough the way he had let his own family down, by not being as available as he should have been in that difficult time.

He'd tried to make up for it since—by returning to Laramie for his residency and taking a permanent job there.

But if he had it to do all over again, he would have done what was right for everyone—not just him.

"That's what I think we should do, too," he said firmly.

"Then it's decided?" Violet asked.

Gavin nodded. The idea of raising a child with such a sweet and sexy woman had been a nice, brief fantasy—but that was all it was; a tantalizing idea. One he was far too practical to waste any time pondering.

"I'll call Mitzy and tell her that we've talked and decided what we want to do."

"WHO KNOWS? THIS might be just the change you've been looking for," Lacey McCabe told Violet two days later.

Violet looked at her mother. An accomplished physician and neonatologist, and head of the pediatrics department at LCH, she had come down to the ambulance bay to await the arrival of baby Ava.

Violet refused to encourage her mother's hope that all six of her daughters would end up with children of their own, in marriages just as solid and strong as hers. "It's just a temporary guardianship, Mom."

"I know you think that now, but babies have a way of latching on to your heart."

"Not in this case," Violet insisted.

She wasn't ready for motherhood.

She certainly wasn't the best choice, long-term, for an orphaned newborn.

But with the help of her family, and Gavin's, she could do the right thing, in the short run. That, she knew.

"Just don't confuse the love you and Gavin will no doubt feel for this child for anything else," her mother continued.

Violet blinked. "Like what?"

Lacey shrugged. "Babies in jeopardy have a way of bringing people together in other ways, too." She paused, concern in her eyes. "Ways that don't last."

Was her mother intimating that she and Gavin would become closer, too, as a consequence? "You don't need to worry about that," Violet huffed, folding her arms across her chest. "Gavin and I know how to work together for the good of a patient—or in this case, a ward—without crossing any boundaries."

Lacey nodded, her maternal gaze cautious. "In any case," she went on, with an approving hug, "I want you to know your father and I are proud of the way you and Gavin are stepping up to take on this unexpected responsibility."

Gavin joined them. He'd been on the midnight-to-noon

ER shift. Clad in surgical scrubs with a shadow of beard on his face, he looked as ruggedly handsome as always. He smiled at Violet and her mom. "Jackson said the same to me a little while ago," he confirmed.

Lacey's dad was not just LCH's chief of staff, he was also famously protective of all six of his daughters. He never hesitated to offer encouragement or to step in with a word of caution if he thought one of them was headed down the wrong path.

"In fact, I think everyone at the hospital is interested in doing what they can for the little one." Gavin hovered closer. "How much longer until they get here?"

Violet dutifully consulted her watch. "Should be any minute now. In fact, Mitzy should be here shortly, too."

Right on cue, the social worker appeared. She had a clipboard full of papers to be signed.

The next few minutes were spent filling out the appropriate paperwork. By the time they'd finished, the ambulance pulled up beneath the portico. The doors opened and the incubator containing baby Ava was brought out. They caught only a distant glimpse of the newborn as she was whisked through a series of corridors that led straight to the Special Care Nursery. "Showtime," Gavin said as they fell into step behind the EMTs.

Was he as nervous about all this as she suddenly was? There was no way to tell. But she was glad he was here with her every step of the way.

Together, Gavin and Violet waited in the corridor outside the unit. Finally, Lacey McCabe came out. Clad in a sterile yellow gown thrown over her clothing, she had a stethoscope around her neck and a smile on her face. "Ava's doing great. You can go in and see her now."

The two of them slipped on yellow gowns and Violet took a bolstering breath as they went inside.

Ava was snuggled on a white flannel blanket that covered the bottom of the enclosed Plexiglas incubator. She had a knit cap on her head, a white knit sweater on her torso that covered her spindly arms and a diaper. Monitors were attached to her chest and foot. She had a nasal cannula to help her get the oxygen she needed.

Her eyes were closed, her dark lashes thick and velvety against her cheeks. She appeared to be sleeping comfortably. Looked sweet and vulnerable. And so very precious, this tiny baby girl.

A lump rose in Violet's throat as she thought about everything the premature infant had already been through. It was one thing to accept responsibility of a child in theory, another to actually do it, live and in person.

Violet let out a tremulous sigh.

Gavin seemed similarly affected. His eyes still on little Ava, he reached over and took Violet's hand in his, giving it a gentle squeeze.

Meg Carrigan, the nursing supervisor, appeared at Violet's elbow. "You can come back and visit her as much as you want, but right now we'd like Ava to rest awhile."

Violet nodded. The doctor in her understood the reasoning. But the "mom" in her wanted to stay. Forever.

Reluctantly, she stepped back.

Gavin took her elbow and led her out of the nursery and into the hall.

A crowd had gathered. Other parents. Staff. Visitors. Everyone wanted a glimpse of the little orphan. Mitzy was there, too, smiling. "Can you believe it?" She was practically gushing as she held up another sheet on her clipboard. "We've already had two dozen families calling, interested in giving her a permanent home. And they haven't even seen her!"

"Great," Violet managed to say, her treacherous heart clenching and unclenching like a fist in the middle of her chest.

Gavin nodded. Tightening his grip on her elbow, he escorted her down the hall and past the elevators, to a deserted corner. "You okay?"

"Wh-what do you mean?"

He edged closer. Head dipping toward hers, he asked quietly, "Are you going to be able to do this?"

Not sure whether to be insulted he doubted her or impressed he could so easily see her inner turmoil, Violet stammered, "O-of course!"

Gavin gave her a probing look that sent heat spiraling through her. "Really? Because, from my view, you already look a little too attached."

HIS OBSERVATION HIT Violet hard, and while Gavin was sorry about that, he also knew it had to be said.

"You had tears in your eyes just now."

She waved a hand. "You were choked up, too."

Only because Violet had been choked up.

Gavin cleared his throat. He saw the vulnerability in her expression and wished there was some way to make this easier for all of them without admitting they might have made a mistake in agreeing to it at all.

Especially if she was this emotionally invested already.

Their eyes met and locked, generating another wave of heat between them. She stepped back slightly, but not before he caught the faint drift of the freesia perfume she favored.

"Look, I'm not going to deny I feel a little sorry for the kid…"

Her golden-brown eyes sparked with indignation. "A little?"

"Okay, a lot." He rested his hands on her shoulders. "Being orphaned is a rough road."

She inhaled shakily, reminding him, "As you very well know from personal experience." Her dark brows knit together. "Which, maybe, is precisely the reason you should be involved?"

Chagrined, he dropped his hold on her. "Temporarily. In a very cursory—guardian in legal aspect only—way." Otherwise, he wasn't sure he could meet this child's needs any better than he had his siblings' in the aftermath of his parents' tragic death.

She gave him an affronted look. "Well, that's not *my* idea of being a guardian."

Out of the corner of his eye he saw several people heading toward them. Figuring this conversation did not need an audience, Gavin cupped Violet's elbow once again, opened the exit door that led to the stairwell and guided her through.

Abruptly, they were surrounded by concrete—and silence. She swung toward him, shivering slightly, her full lips slanting downward. "You can't get emotionally attached to this baby, Violet."

"Actually, I can't *not* have feelings for her."

Watching a shadow cross her face, he wanted to protect her all the more. "You know what I mean."

Violet folded her arms in front of her, the action pushing up the soft swell of her breasts. She released another long, quavering breath. "You think I should handle the situation the way you do your ER patients?" Clearly aware this situation was becoming far too intimate too fast, she paced away from him. Leaning against the wall, she propped her hands on the railing behind her. "Treat 'em and street 'em?"

Not about to apologize for doing his job, and doing it well, he replied in a low, matter-of-fact voice, "Patients come in. They have a medical problem that needs to be dealt with. I diagnose it, administer the proper care and then wish them well as they head either out the door or to another floor of the hospital."

"In any case," she accused, "you don't have to see them again or get emotionally involved."

"Actually," Gavin corrected, matching her high-brow tone, "some of them I do see on a rather regular basis. Anyone with a chronic health problem. Cystic fibrosis, cancer and congestive heart failure patients tend to come into the ER at least once or twice a year, if not more, depending on the situation."

She moved to sit on the floor and propped her folded arms on her upraised knees. "Okay. I'll grant you that."

He sat next to her; so close their legs almost touched. "I never give anyone less than my best. It still doesn't mean, however, that I'm unnecessarily involved with my patients." The way, he observed silently, she often seemed to be.

"Well, that's true." Violet rubbed at an imaginary spot on her jeans. "You do have a rep for having a barbed-wired heart."

Her teasing tone did little to allay the sting of the words. He elbowed her playfully. "Actually, Penelope said I didn't have a romantic bone in my body."

"What did you do to make her think that?"

Pushing aside the memory of the bitter breakup, he shrugged. "I think it's more what I refused to do."

Interest lit her curious eyes. "Which was...?"

"Sugarcoat anything. Life is what it is." Fate had taught him that. "I'm not going to pretend otherwise."

Violet pivoted to face him, her bent knee nudging his thigh.

Trying not to think what it would feel like to have the rest of her touching him, in a much more intimate way, he admitted wryly, "I think the consensus is that I'm 'emotionally unavailable.' And therefore, profoundly undatable."

She tilted her head and then rose slowly, dusting off the seat of her pants.

He noticed she didn't argue the assessment.

"That's too bad. Everyone should have a great love at least once in their life." Were they flirting? It seemed as if they were.

He got to his feet, too. Glad to once again be towering over her. "At thirty-two, I hardly think my time has come and gone."

Violet laughed, suddenly looking a whole lot more relaxed. "True. I suppose there's still a *chance* you'll open up in here." She tapped his heart.

He quirked a brow. "Or not."

She was about to say something else when his phone beeped. He read the text message, then said, "I'm needed in the ER." He paused in surprise as another text followed. "And so are you."

Chapter Three

The paramedics had just finished wheeling the gurney holding eighty-two-year-old Carlson Willoughby into an exam bay when Violet and Gavin walked in.

As usual, Violet noted, his wife, Wanda, was by his side. Both were dressed in tracksuits that zipped up the front. Hers was pink and white; his, a jaunty navy blue.

"Hey, Dr. McCabe." Carlson lifted a hand weakly in greeting. As always, he was impeccably clean-shaven, but his thinning, snow-white hair was damp with what appeared to be sweat.

Violet grinned at one of her favorite patients. "Back again?"

He grimaced. "Unfortunately."

The paramedic handed Violet a chart. "He collapsed with pain on his lower right side. Because of his history, we felt it best to bring him in."

"A lot of fuss over nothing," Carlson grumbled, glaring at his IV. He winked at his wife. "Although I do enjoy an ambulance ride from time to time."

"This is no joking matter, Carlson," Wanda chided.

"Everything is a joking matter," he returned with an affable grin.

"No fever," the nurse taking his vitals said. "BP 140 over 100, heart rate 98."

Gavin stepped in, as attending ER physician, to do the

physical exam. "So what else has been going on?" he asked while palpitating the older man's abdomen.

Violet noted Carlson seemed to be in pain.

"He's had stomach issues the past few days," his wife explained.

Carlson waved off the concern. "It was probably my cooking. I tried a new recipe as a surprise on our sixtieth wedding anniversary."

"Congratulations." Violet smiled, impressed at the longevity of their relationship.

Wanda told her husband, "Your tendency to overspice everything has nothing to do with this. If it did, you would be sick all the time."

Carlson guffawed.

"Anything else of note?" Gavin asked, frowning as he checked the lymph nodes.

Carlson was mum.

"He's had pain," his wife declared. "I know he has for weeks now. He just won't admit it."

"Everyone our age has pain."

Wanda dabbed her eyes. "I think the cancer has returned."

Violet hoped that was not the case. She'd become very close to the older couple over the past five years. Too close, she sometimes thought.

"Which was why I asked for you." Carlson looked pointedly at Violet. "I want you to tell Wanda that's just not true."

Violet forced a matter-of-fact smile.

"All this is, is old age and indigestion," the patient declared stalwartly. "Tell her, Dr. McCabe."

Violet wished it was that simple. "You know I can't rule anything out from an oncology perspective until we do a few tests. Which you are about due for, anyway, aren't you?"

Carlson groaned at the prospect. Defiantly, he attempted to sit up and shook his head. "Now that I've celebrated our anniversary here—"

Gavin gave the couple a curious look.

"We met in the ER sixty years ago, fell in love at first sight and married a week later," Wanda explained. She patted her husband's hand fondly. "And I have never regretted loving this man for an instant."

"Nor I you. And now that we've commemorated that great day with yet another trip to the hospital, I just want to go home," Carlson said stubbornly.

"And you will. In a day or so. After we make sure everything is as it should be," Violet said soothingly.

Briefly, she and Gavin stepped out to consult and then she returned to the exam room. "Dr. Monroe confirms you are in no immediate danger. However, we both think you need more tests. So I'm admitting you on the oncology floor."

"Thank heaven." Wanda exhaled in relief.

Carlson scowled in mock aggravation. "Don't be so anxious to get rid of me!"

"Hey," Wanda replied, her usual good cheer returning now that her husband was in good hands. "Even I deserve a Carlson-free evening every now and then." She winked at her beloved. "So stop trying to ruin it for me!"

The couple chuckled in unison. Their verbal one-upmanship continued, to the amusement of the staff.

Grinning, Violet stepped out to the nurses' station to write the orders.

By the time she had finished, Carlson was already on his way up to a private room. Gavin had been called to stitch up a teenager who had accidentally thrown a baseball through a window, then cut his hand while cleaning up the broken glass.

And that was when one of his sisters, Bridgette, rushed through the emergency entrance.

She and her twin, Bess, were both nurses. But only Bridgette had returned to Laramie to live.

A nurse in the neonatal unit, the lively twenty-four-year-old brunette was usually enviably calm.

Not today.

In paint-splattered clothing, her keys in one hand, cell phone in the other, she strode toward the desk. "Where's Gavin?"

"With a patient. What's going on?"

"It's Nicholas." Violet knew she was referring to their nineteen-year-old brother. "He was in an accident."

"Oh, no! Is he hurt?"

"I'm not sure. I got a call they're bringing him in."

In the distance, sirens sounded. Bridgette looked around, wild-eyed and teary.

"I'll get Gavin," Violet told her.

She grabbed a pair of sterile gloves as she walked through the exam room door. "Want me to finish up?" she said with a look that told Gavin he was needed elsewhere.

"Sure." He handed off the task to her.

By the time Violet had finished with the stitches, the EMTs were wheeling Nicholas in on a gurney.

If the way he was arguing with the EMTs was any indication, she thought, he wasn't badly hurt.

"—completely unnecessary."

"Your pickup rolled and nearly went down a ravine. You're getting checked out."

Another ER doc followed the gurney into an exam room. She came out ten minutes later, announcing, "Except for a few bruises, he's fine."

"Thank heaven." Bridgette sighed, rushing in, Gavin beside her.

Seconds later, sounds of arguing could be heard.

Knowing if it continued, other patients would be disturbed, Violet knocked on the door and breezed in. "How's it going here?"

Nicholas looked at Violet and pointed at his two older siblings. "Tell them I have every right to drop out of college if that's what I want."

What?

Gavin gave Violet a look that said "Help me out here..."

She smiled. "Is this really the time and place to have this discussion? Because there are others in the waiting room still needing to be seen. So..."

"Violet's right." Bridgette looked at her younger brother. "I'll drive you home."

"I'll take care of the paperwork," Gavin said.

"Are you okay?" Violet asked gently after his two siblings had left.

Gavin rubbed a hand over his face.

For the first time she realized what it must have been like for him when his parents died.

Gavin had been about to enter medical school but his twin sisters and younger brother had still been in their teens. It had been up to Gavin and his older sister, Erin, who had been married with kids of her own, to finish raising them. Plus, manage the family's ranch and Western wear store in town. Erin had insisted Gavin continue with his education, rather than forgo his dreams, and after some initial arguing about whether that was too much for his older sister to handle on her own, he had. He'd returned every few months to help out. And done his best to keep in touch, in between visits, but it couldn't have been easy for any of them.

Yet never once had she heard Gavin complain.

Gavin dropped his hand to his side. "Yeah. It's just the accident talking. He'll be okay when he calms down and comes to his senses."

"Is there anything else I can do?"

Gavin shook his head. "Thanks for offering." He inhaled. "I better call Erin, though. Before she hears about it from anyone else."

Violet watched him leave with newfound respect. For reasons she couldn't really explain, she was tempted to stay around awhile anyway to make sure Gavin was really okay in the wake of the traumatic event. Offer comfort. Take him to lunch. Something. But that was ridiculous, she knew. The two of them didn't have that kind of relationship. They were casual friends, nothing more. If Gavin needed to turn to someone for support, it wouldn't be to her.

Meanwhile, there were places she was needed. She had things to do at McCabe House. She also wanted to check on Ava before she left the hospital.

To her relief, the newborn was sleeping peacefully.

Meg Carrigan joined her at the incubator. "Funny," the sixty-year-old nursing supervisor mused, "how easily these little ones grab our hearts and then hold on with all their might."

Which was considerable, Violet thought. She turned to the trim redhead, who was also a dear family friend. "It still gets to you after all these years?"

Meg nodded. She patted Violet's shoulder. "Luckily, as each one of these little darlings leaves, another arrives, needing just as much TLC."

That was true, Violet thought, for the nurses and doctors in NICU. It wouldn't necessarily hold for her. And that was a good thing. Thus far, despite the fact that all her sisters now had families of their own—or in Poppy's case, was actively planning one—she had yet to catch baby fever.

Given the fact she'd already had—and lost—the love of her life, she preferred it to stay that way.

FIVE HOURS LATER Violet opened a window on the second floor of McCabe House. She leaned out, video camera in hand, just in time to see Gavin getting out of his pickup.

He was wearing faded denim jeans, boots and an old button-down shirt, the shirttails hanging out. His clothes looked as comfortable and broken in as her favorite pair of flannel pajamas.

She let her gaze rove his tousled dark hair, broad shoulders and sandpaper hint of beard lining his handsome face. "I didn't expect to see you again today."

At 6:00 p.m. she'd expected him to be headed home to bed after pulling the twelve-hour ER shift the previous day, then staying on to help out through most of the afternoon.

He reached into his truck for a file folder, then flashed her a brief smile. "Mitzy stopped me on the way out of the hospital. She wants us to fill out some questionnaires on what we're looking for in adoptive parents for Ava."

"You didn't have to bring it all the way out here."

"She wants us in agreement on the answers before she sees them. I figured it would be easier to do it in person than on the phone."

Violet wasn't sure she understood his logic. Except that doing it in person would allow them the opportunity to gage the expressions on each other's face to more effectively read their mood.

Not that Gavin was helping her out right now with that. His handsome face was poker-inscrutable. As always.

She sighed, not sure why the fact he was such a mystery was so frustrating to her.

Pushing aside her pique, she asked, "Do you have to work tonight?"

He shook his head. "I don't go in until midnight tomorrow. But if this is a bad time…"

Truth be told she had nothing ahead of her that evening but finishing her current chore and trying to restore order to the mess she'd made of her Conestoga wagon bedroom that morning. "It's not. I just need to finish what I'm doing here. You can come on up, if you want. The front door is open."

She backed out of the window and by the time she had it shut and locked, he was standing in the room, looking like a dark angel in the fading sunlight pouring in through the glass.

As he strode closer, she drank him in from head to toe. Up close, she could see how tired he looked around the eyes. Her heart went out to him. She knew how it felt to come off a long shift. She also knew what it took to keep going and to do what had to be done, regardless of bone-deep fatigue. It was something they'd learned in med school and never forgot.

He inclined his head at the camera in her hand. "What are you filming?"

"The interior of the house, pre-renovation. My sister Callie—"

"The marketing and social media whiz?"

Violet nodded, impressed he could keep all five of her sisters straight. Not everyone could. "She's going to put together a short film about my late grandparents. Show how they started the hospital as physician and nurse and helped build it into the state-of-the-art county medical facility it is today."

He fell into step beside her. "I know they were active on the board of directors, even after they retired."

Proudly, Violet admitted, "John and Lilah helped raise a lot of money to add oncology, neonatal intensive care and cardio-pulmonary care, as well as the medical residency programs for all three. Turning this ranch into living quarters for families dealing with medical crises was their last wish." She took a breath. "And although they left enough money in their estate to redo the house, and eventually the stable-house, where I'm currently staying— which will eventually house the new director—we'll need to raise more money if we're to expand and keep it going as a nonprofit."

He folded his arms in front of him, the action delineating the strong musculature of his chest. "And that is where the video comes in."

"We'll use it to show exactly where the money is going and how much good any donation does." Violet moved along the hall, filming the empty rooms with the faded paint and wallpaper.

He gave her enough room to work unencumbered. "So when does the construction start?"

Determined not to let him see how much his nearness affected her, Violet raised a blind to let more light into the last room. "They're bringing the Dumpster tomorrow morning. Once it's set up, the teardown of the interior will begin."

"Sounds noisy." Finished, she turned off the camera and led the way downstairs. "That's why they make noise-canceling headphones. Luckily—" she winked as she locked up and led the way across the yard to the stable-house "—I brought along a pair. And extra batteries, too."

Chuckling at her sassy tone, he followed her into the stable-house.

His brow lifted at what he found. "Wow. You've been busy."

ALTHOUGH WHY, GAVIN THOUGHT, she wanted to be stranded out here, away from all her family and friends, still puzzled him. Was she running away from something? Trying to get her thoughts together? Or fulfilling some cockeyed notion of the McCabe clan's famous Texas Pioneer spirit?

Hard to say.

But whatever was going on with Violet, she was clearly determined to make it work, at least for the next few months. "It's a big improvement over the way it looked two days ago," he continued, impressed.

All the moving boxes had been pushed to the rear of the former stable and were neatly lined up behind the Conestoga wagon that functioned as her bedroom.

On the right side of the large space she had rolled a rug out over the painted concrete floor and arranged a sofa, armchair and two end tables to make a nice conversation area. A big packing trunk served as a coffee table.

On the other side of the room a wooden trestle table provided additional kitchen counter space. It held a microwave, toaster oven and what looked like an electric skillet. The small refrigerator stood next to that. A white wrought-iron patio set now served as the dining room table and chairs.

There were no shades or drapes on the tall casement windows that lined either side of the room, which was where she had placed the Conestoga wagon. Its rounded, white-canvas top would come in handy, he realized, since the flaps could be tied shut on either end, allowing her complete privacy. For changing and—

He didn't need to be thinking about that.

What she wore—or didn't wear—to sleep in was none of his business.

Violet looked at the dusky light outside and switched on the overhead lights. Mounted close to the ceiling, they let off the kind of bright fluorescence the hospital corridors afforded. A bonus, given the fact he was a little too interested in the way her thigh-length shorts, faded college T-shirt and sneakers cloaked her spectacular body.

"Do you have the questionnaires?" she asked brusquely, bringing his attention back to where it needed to be once again.

He lifted the manila file amiably. "Right here."

A faint blush highlighted the elegant contours of her

cheeks. She looked around until she found something to write with. "A pen?"

Gavin patted his pocket. Found his cell phone but nothing else. "Ah, no."

"No problem. I think I have some extra in my bedside drawer. I'll be right back." She headed up the stairs and disappeared into the covered wagon.

While Gavin waited, he checked out the ventilation in the room, which seemed comfortably cool despite the warmth of the summer day. Further investigation showed why. Long-handled cranks opened the tall, abundant windows along the very top quarter of the glass. The ceiling fan whirred overhead, cooling and dispersing the fresh air. As a result, the room smelled like the sunny autumn day it had been. Fresh and clean, like the great Texas outdoors.

He could see why she liked it out here, although it had to be lonely, too, he thought. Especially at night.

Almost too quiet.

In the wagon, however, it was anything but.

He could hear things being shifted, occasional muttering and…was that swearing? There was a small crash, a shift of bedsprings and then an even bigger crash.

Followed only by silence.

Gavin waited.

Still nothing.

He began to get a little worried. "Violet? You okay in there?"

The bedsprings creaked.

There was a muffled cry.

"Violet?" he called out again.

And then he heard what sounded like a small, furious scream. *What the…?*

Gavin took the steps up to the wagon two at a time. He threw back the flap that hid the interior from view.

Violet lay facedown on the bed, her head burrowed in

the pillow, one arm tucked awkwardly between the mattress and the end table next to it.

"What the heck are you doing?"

She moaned and lifted her head slightly. "I'm stuck."

"STUCK," GAVIN REPEATED STUPIDLY.

"I had a box of pens and pencils and I knocked them behind the nightstand. I was trying to reach it without moving all my suitcases, storage boxes and garment bags."

Of which, Gavin noted, there were many. All crammed together in the available space between the mattress and the high wooden sides of the wagon.

He tracked the silky dark mane over her face and shoulders. "You're really stuck?"

She groaned again and pounded her forehead lightly against the mattress beneath her. "No. I'm just lying here for the fun of it."

He grinned. A sensually indisposed Violet was a sight to behold. Her temper only added to the allure. "Hang on." He sprang into action. "I'll move some of these suitcases."

A feat that was easier said than done, he quickly discovered. Some boxes were wedged in there pretty tight. Plus, the stack was two and three high on all sides. "What did you pack in these, anyway?" He succeeded in freeing a storage box from the stack, only to have the snapped lid fly off in the process and a whole array of sexy undies come spilling out. About half of which landed on her shoulders and head.

Another string of muffled, surprisingly unladylike profanities filled the silence. She turned her face to his. "Did you do that on purpose?"

"Ah, no." The last thing he needed to see was what kind of undergarments she wore. Now he'd be imagining how she looked in all that sexy satin and lace. "Sorry." He rescued the rest of her undies and stuffed them all back in the box, snapping the lid on.

"Are these all clothes?"

"Yes. It's everything I might need for the next three months and then some."

"Sounds like a woman." His sisters were notorious clothes-hounds, too.

"And spoken like a man. Are you hurrying?"

Gavin lifted another box of undies and a half-open suitcase of what appeared to be silk pajamas and nightgowns. Who knew she dressed so sexily when she wasn't at the hospital? Except, in the past five years, she had almost always been at the hospital.

"Gavin?"

"Almost there."

She moaned.

He shifted the suitcase wedged against the side of the queen-size mattress and the wagon.

She tried to pull free. Groaned again, in what seemed to be real pain this time. "Still stuck…"

No kidding. Her arm remained clamped tight between the nightstand and the bed.

Deftly, Gavin slid one arm between her and the mattress, simultaneously pushing down on the bed while supporting the weight of her chest. Then, still supporting her weight and keeping her trapped arm in place, he used his free hand to shove the mattress several inches away from the nightstand, toward the other side of the wagon.

That gave her just enough wiggle room.

Her breasts pearling tautly against his forearm, she pulled her trapped limb free and rolled onto her back. Rubbing from shoulder to elbow to wrist, she tested the flexibility of her fingers with a beleaguered sigh. "Wow, that hurt!"

"Are you sure you're okay?"

She sat up, still rubbing the affected limb. Beneath her shirt, he couldn't help but note her breasts were still taut.

Oblivious to his wicked thoughts, she scoffed playfully. "You mean aside from my wounded pride?"

Glad she hadn't lost her sense of humor, he grinned and sank down on the bed. He felt the drumbeat of arousal as he faced her. "I kind of like you as a damsel in distress."

She crossed her arms over her breasts, her delicate hands resting on opposite shoulders, at the nape of her neck. "You are so funny."

Suddenly sensing she needed more comforting than her self-imposed hug could give, he shifted closer. "I'm serious, Violet," he said softly.

And then he did what he'd been wanting to do since forever. He took her into his arms, tilted her face up to his and kissed her.

Chapter Four

Violet wanted to say she was surprised. That she hadn't expected Gavin to ever kiss her. But that would not be true.

She could tell by the way he had been looking at her the past day or so that he had been considering doing just that.

What was worse, she had been feeling the exact same urge.

She didn't know whether it was the fact they suddenly both found themselves responsible for baby Ava's future, or the fact that Gavin was just so damn sexy. All she knew for sure was that when he'd come to her rescue and slid his brawny arm beneath her, her body had responded with a lightning bolt of desire that had started in her breasts and exploded like a thundercloud inside her. And now that he was kissing her, a second, even more powerful wave had started to surge. Driven, this time, by the hot, ardent press of his lips and the evocative sweep of his tongue.

He tasted so incredibly good, she realized as her eyes fluttered shut. Like mint and man, desire and determination. And it wasn't just physical need he was conjuring up. There was a sudden riptide of long-suppressed feelings, too. The fact she had been alone, too long. An aching awareness of just how lost she had been and a deep, bolstering need for more...

And still Gavin kissed her, tangling her tongue with his, arousing even more passion and need. With a sound that was half whimper of protest, half sigh of submission, she allowed him to unwind her hands from her shoulders and drape them over the broad width of his. She let him fit his chest to hers and then, the next thing she knew, he altered her center of balance. She was sliding sideways on the bed. He was shifting her onto her back, moving over her, his hands cupping her breasts, his thumbs moving erotically across the crests. And, dear heaven, that felt so…darn…good, too.

Violet groaned again.

If they kept this up, they would make love.

And she knew—for so many reasons, baby Ava among the most important of them—she could not let that happen.

The situation was confused enough as it was.

With a soft whimper she put both hands on his shoulders, broke the kiss and pushed him away.

GAVIN OPENED HIS EYES and shifted onto his side, unsure whether Violet looked relieved or disappointed he had stopped.

He knew he was both.

For as much as he wanted to make love to her right here and now, the more pragmatic part of him knew that doing so would have been a colossal mistake.

Violet was the most idealistic woman he had ever met.

She believed in love with all her heart and soul.

Not hookups.

Not tawdry one-night stands.

When she made love with a man again—and he was determined now, after kissing her, that it *would* be with him—she would want it to mean something.

The surprise was that he wanted their coming together to mean something, too.

She took a conciliatory breath. "I'm sorry," she said.

Gavin grinned, aware he was enjoying spending time

with her more than he had enjoyed anything in a long time. "For what? Kissing me back?"

Violet shook her head as if that would get her back on track and locked eyes with him. "No. For doing whatever it was I did to lead you on."

Ah. So this is the way she's going to play it.

She straightened, her face still flushed with desire, and scooted her hips to the foot of the bed.

"You didn't lead me on," he said, testing her, too.

She glanced back at him, her tousled hair enticingly spilling over her shoulders.

Resisting the urge to run his hands through the silky strands, he concentrated on the just-kissed softness of her lips before returning his attention to her eyes. "You've always made it clear you're still in love with Sterling."

There was a long, thoughtful pause that seemed to indicate he had guessed wrong about that.

Finally, she tilted her head. "Then you do understand."

He had the distinct impression they were talking about two different things.

"Frankly, I'm envious." Gavin was prodding, trying to figure out what exactly was holding her back if not her love for her late fiancé. "He was a lucky guy."

Violet slid off the edge of the bed. "Until he died when he was twenty-five."

Gavin swore silently. He had a habit of saying the wrong thing at the wrong time in these kinds of situations. He stood, too. "You know what I mean."

"I just don't like it when people tell me how great we had it. Or how lucky we were to have found each other. Because nothing about it feels lucky, Gavin." She paused, her lower lip quivering.

"I'm sorry," he said, quietly pulling her into his arms and giving her the hug she seemed to need.

For an instant she sank into him. When she pulled back,

there were tears shimmering in her eyes. "Forget all the books and movies, Gavin," she whispered. "There's nothing romantic about having a terminal illness. For the patient, or his or her loved ones." She swallowed, pressing a palm to her forehead. "It just…"

"Sucks. I know. And I am sorry. For wanting to understand and not being able to because I haven't walked a mile in your shoes."

Again their eyes met. This time she accepted his acknowledgment of her pain.

After a moment her expression changed and she took a deep breath and forced a smile. "Moving on…" She brushed past him, to the narrow aisle he had created. "I still forgot to get pens!" This time when she reached down between the mattress and nightstand, there was just enough room. She bounded back up, plastic box filled with writing utensils clasped in hand. "Now, on to what we should be doing. Filling out those questionnaires…"

"WHY NOT ADMIT you made a mistake with this whole glamping thing and move in with me temporarily," Violet's oldest sister, Poppy, said the next day when she arrived to assess Violet's storage needs. Fiercely independent, and the only single-birthed daughter of Jackson and Lacey McCabe—who also boasted a set of twins and triplet daughters—Poppy was an interior designer, known for her practicality, efficiency and style.

"I just need a neat and inexpensive way to organize my clothes so I'm not tripping over them or rooting through boxes and suitcases for the next few months."

And, Violet thought, still getting hot and bothered whenever she thought about it, she *especially* didn't need to be rolling around on her bed kissing Gavin Monroe! Not that she was obsessing over their hot, sexy clinch or anything.

Poppy walked around the large space, measuring, thinking, making notes. She swung back around. "I have plenty of room in my bungalow, you know."

Violet looked at the gray clouds on the horizon. "Thanks, sis, but I'd rather be here."

Poppy frowned. "Aren't you lonely?"

She sure hadn't been last night. Gavin had stayed another hour and a half, as they'd taken their time with the questionnaires, debating each fine point, wondering what would be best for their tiny charge.

But at least he hadn't tried to kiss her again when he left—

The sound of a big tractor-trailer roaring up the lane jerked Violet from her reverie.

She and Poppy moved to the open screen door. They looked out to see the arrival of the big steel Dumpster for the construction debris, and another six pickup trucks carrying the workers.

"I mean, it's so quiet out here in off-hours. And it looks like it's going to be really noisy during work hours."

"I can handle that." Violet pointed to her headphones. "As for the rest of the time, I like my solitude."

Her sister's gaze narrowed. "Too much sometimes?"

Everyone had thought that, after Sterling died. What they hadn't understood was how much the alone time had helped Violet to process her loss and work through not only her grief but the many mistakes she had made, the countless ways she had let Sterling down.

Now, finally, she was ready to move on.

She just wasn't sure to where or to what.

All she knew for sure was that she felt stuck. And the only way to get out of her rut was to seek change. Big, life-altering change. In the meantime, though…

"I have the transformation of McCabe House to keep

me occupied." She glanced at her watch. "And I have to get to the hospital, too."

"To check on the baby you and Gavin are temporary guardians for?"

Violet nodded, aware that with the exception of the four phone calls she'd made to the nurses' station in the Special Care Nursery, she had sort of been delaying going back there in person. For reasons she didn't really understand.

"I don't suppose there's any chance the baby could go to a couple who isn't married?"

Violet knew that Poppy and her best friend, the currently deployed Lieutenant Trace Caulder, were trying to adopt—without getting married.

"The mother's wishes were clear. She wanted her baby to have a mother and a father who are in a committed relationship, if possible." She continued walking around with her older sister, showing her the space. "So Gavin and I talked it over and decided it would be best if Ava went to a married couple with an established family unit."

Poppy stopped to measure a length of windowless wall. "Which would put me and Trace out of the running, since the good lieutenant isn't due back in the United States for a visit for another ten months or so." She sighed wistfully.

Violet held one end of the tape measure for her. "Ava needs new parents as soon as possible. Luckily, Mitzy is expediting the process. So it all should happen fairly quickly."

"It's a good thing that, unlike me, you don't fall completely in love with every infant you see."

Violet bit her lip. Truth was, the pang of longing she'd felt deep inside when she'd gotten her first glimpse of little Ava had caught her completely off guard. And she hadn't even held her in her arms yet!

But, for obvious reasons, she wasn't *about* to admit that to her sister.

Poppy jotted down a final set of numbers. She looked back up, a fleeting sadness in her eyes as the two of them strolled toward the door. "Anyway, back to your current storage problem… I'll pull a solution together for you and then let you know what we're going to need."

"Thanks, Poppy." Violet gave her big sister a hug and watched as she drove off. She signed off on the delivery of the Dumpster, talked to the construction foreman, then headed into town, the completed questionnaires in tow.

Mitzy was out on a home visit, so she left the paperwork at her office, then went on to the hospital. Carlson Willoughby was undergoing the first of several days of testing. Since the results weren't yet in, she went up to the nursery to check on their charge and caught her breath at what she saw.

Gavin, sitting beside the incubator, a blanket-wrapped baby Ava cuddled gently in his arms. The tiny infant had a pink cap on her head, a nasal cannula still assisting her breathing, monitors that measured her heartbeat and breathing visible beneath the soft white blanket that surrounded her.

Her eyes were shut and she appeared to be sleeping.

Violet could hardly blame her.

To be held against that strong, warm chest, cradled so tenderly by those brawny arms…

Violet grabbed a sterile gown, put it on over her clothes and slipped into the small, dimly lit visiting room behind the glass window.

"Hey," she said softly.

Gavin looked up at her. "The nurses wanted me to hold her for a little bit."

She ambled closer. "I can see that."

The tenderness in his expression made him all the more handsome. "I have to admit, I never really understood why the parents of premature infants were so loath to leave the nursery and head home to rest."

She nodded, trying to swallow past the lump in her throat. "But you get it now."

He shot her a knowing grin. "You should give it a try."

"I don't want to interrupt..."

He stood and gestured toward the comfortable recliner-rocker he'd been sitting in.

Unable to summon a reason why she shouldn't start fulfilling her duties as temporary guardian, too, Violet took his place in the seat that still held his warmth. And the enticing soap-and-man scent of his skin.

Gently, he transferred Ava to her arms.

The preemie was incredibly light and fragile, at just a little more than four pounds. As Violet looked down at Ava, a wave of tenderness unlike anything she had ever felt swept through her.

Gavin pulled another chair up to sit beside Violet. Together, they watched the sleeping baby. Neither speaking. Barely moving. Yet united just the same.

Who knew how long they would have stayed that way had Bridgette, the nurse on duty, not come in to reluctantly interrupt. "It's time to put Ava back in the warmer. But if you'd like to come back later this evening to help us try to get her started on drinking formula from a bottle, that would be great."

Gavin and Violet exchanged looks. "I'll be here," Violet said.

To her surprise Gavin said gruffly, "So will I."

Bridgette nodded, accepting the news with the same equanimity she accepted the infant. Bridgette looked at her big brother. "Would you mind hanging around for a moment? I really need to talk to you about Nicholas. And, Violet, if you've got a moment, I'd like your opinion, too."

As soon as Ava was settled, Bridgette told her coworkers she was taking her break.

The three of them headed for the staff lounge, which was blissfully empty. Although not sure what she might have to contribute in what seemed to be a Monroe family matter, Violet was glad to be of assistance in any way that she could.

Violet and Gavin both got coffee, while Bridgette grabbed a bottle of water. "Nicholas rented a car and went back to Austin this morning," she said.

"That's good," Gavin said.

Bridgette took a seat on the sofa. Violet settled opposite her, and Gavin sank down beside her, close enough she was aware of his steady male presence but not close enough to be touching.

His sister looked worried. "I'm not so sure. He hasn't been the same since the accident."

Gavin's brow furrowed. "Medically?"

"Emotionally," Bridgette corrected. "Swerving to avoid running over that deer changed him. He said he saw his life flash before his eyes. And he didn't like what he saw. So far, anyway."

"What's that supposed to mean?" Gavin chided.

"I don't know. But I have this uneasy sense that he's planning something." Bridgette turned to Violet. "You have a lot of experience with young adult patients coming close to the brink, then recovering and trying to resume a normal life. Does that seem like a common reaction to you?"

Reluctantly, Violet admitted, "If something's brewing in a person, yes, it usually erupts under the stress." As it had with Sterling.

Gavin turned to her, his shoulder nudging hers in the process. "What should we do?"

What I didn't, Violet thought before she answered.

"Listen to whatever your brother has to say. And take Nicholas seriously—even if it seems like he's coming out of left field."

Gavin promised Bridgette, "I'll give him a call later this evening…see if he'll tell me what's on his mind."

"I'm sure he'll appreciate it," Bridgette said, standing.

The three of them said goodbye and Bridgette went back to work. Gavin and Violet left the staff lounge.

"So what now?" Gavin said as they walked toward the elevator.

Violet hated to admit just how at loose ends she was. After five years of residency, never having a moment to spare, this barely working at all would get old fast. Even if she was still trying to figure out what the next phase of her life held.

She punched the down button. "As far as work goes, I'm still waiting on the results of Carlson Willoughby's tests, but otherwise I'm not on call today so—" Violet's phone vibrated.

When she looked at the screen, there was an email from her sister. Reading it quickly, Violet groaned.

"Problem?" Gavin asked, rocking forward on his toes and hooking his thumbs through the denim loops on either side of his fly.

The elevator arrived and the door opened. It was a little crowded, so they had no choice but to squeeze together to avoid stepping on other passengers.

The warmth of his body sent a new flood of desire through her. "Poppy is going to set me up with a movable wardrobe system, but I'm going to have to drive to a store in San Angelo to pick up the components."

The elevator opened up on the lobby. "Will you be able to fit it all in your SUV?"

Violet hesitated, unsure.

Gavin gestured gallantly. "My truck is available. As am I."

Was he hitting on her? Or just being helpful? Hard to tell. "You'd really want to do that on your day off?"

His grin widened. "Sure. If you buy me lunch first."

She couldn't help it. She laughed. "I take it you have a place in mind."

He fell into step beside her as they headed outside into the gloomy autumn day. "I do."

To ensure they would be able to cart everything back to Laramie, they drove separately and ended up at a popular Mexican restaurant in San Angelo. Violet ordered the enchiladas supreme and he followed suit.

"I didn't know you were a fan of enchiladas," she teased as they dug in to their combination plate of chicken, cheese, beef and bean enchiladas, accompanied by a side of Mexican rice.

"I'm trying to expand my horizons."

"Away from steak fajitas?" Which, she knew, from attending the same hospital staff luncheons for the past five years, happened to be his favorite. Not that she had been noticing or anything.

"In a lot of ways."

His expression was both deadpan and mysterious. So why was she thinking about kissing him again? And why was he suddenly looking a tad uncomfortable, too?

"So, about those questionnaires we filled out last night…" He swallowed and took a long thirsty drink of iced tea. "Do you really think the age cutoff for applicants should be thirty-five instead of forty?"

Back to Ava and their joint responsibility, which was where their attention should be. Violet met his eyes, her mood suddenly introspective. "You think twenty-five to thirty-five is too narrow a range for prospective parents?"

"I don't want to go any younger, but I don't think it

would hurt to go a little older. There's something to be said for maturity."

She nodded tensely.

His blue gaze roved her face. "You don't look happy."

Her appetite fading, Violet put her fork down. "It's a big decision."

"We'll find the right family," Gavin promised as an intimate silence descended between them.

"You sound so sure."

He quirked a brow. "You doubt that?"

Violet sat back in her chair. "On an intellectual level I know that, statistically, given how many people there are in this county alone who are ready, willing and able to adopt a newborn child, it should be no problem to find a home for Ava."

"But?" He finished his iced tea in a single draught.

"Knowing that doesn't make the prospect of selecting parents for Ava any easier." It was such an overwhelming responsibility! More so since she'd actually met the precious newborn and held her in her arms.

Gavin touched her hand.

Violet swallowed and pushed on around the sudden parched feeling in her throat. "What if we choose the wrong family? What if there are too many potential adoptive parents who fit the criteria perfectly? How will we choose just one set of parents without feeling like we are somehow being unfair to whoever didn't get chosen?"

He shrugged, let go of her hand and sat back, too. "How about we cross that bridge when we get to it?"

"You're right. I know that." She sighed as the waitress delivered their check.

And, as promised, Violet paid it.

Luckily, they now had things to do to keep them busy.

The wardrobe components, which were supposed to be ready for her, had not yet been pulled off the shelf. So she and Gavin went around the store with a flatbed-style cart, selecting the appropriate shelving and hardware.

"How many clothes do you have?" he asked with a bemused smile.

Aware she'd gotten everything she needed, Violet took a place in one of the checkout lines. Gavin stood behind her. "You saw them last night. All those suitcases, plastic storage containers and duffel bags around my bed."

He stacked the heavy boxes containing the movable closet onto the end of the conveyer belt. "Ah, yes, the feminine mess of it all."

Violet set the accessories on top, then turned to him as they waited for the customer in front of them to finish. She propped her hands on her waist. "Excuse me?"

He waggled his brows, teasing, "I've got three sisters. I know what it looks like when they have a wardrobe crisis."

Guilty as charged, unfortunately.

Flushing, Violet added more accessories to the conveyer belt. "I wasn't having one," she fibbed, unwilling to admit how the crisis she was having had spread to all areas of her life. "I just lugged the stuff up there so I could lay it all out on my bed and sort through it. Which I started to do this morning—"

"Meaning it's even more cluttered now than it was last night?"

The young male clerk grinned as he finished ringing them up.

Violet gave an indignant sniff. "I couldn't find what I wanted to wear to the hospital this morning. And I was in a hurry to get there." She handed over her credit card, then stepped up to sign.

Finished, she took the receipt, smiled and thanked the clerk, then followed Gavin out the automatic doors to the parking lot.

Aware how cozy and right this was all beginning to feel,

she stopped at the tail ends of their vehicles and picked up the threads of the conversation as she opened her SUV. "Although I would have rushed even more had I known I was going to have the opportunity to hold Ava for the first time this morning."

He paused in lowering his tailgate and turned to her, an expression of unbearable tenderness on his handsome face. "It was a moment," he admitted with surprising reverence.

Violet wasn't surprised to hear Gavin admit that. He was compassionate, as well as practical and forthright, down to his very soul.

She *was* surprised, however, to see him look so personally affected. He'd never been one to lust after having kids, the way some guys his age did. Yet in this particular instant, she could almost swear he'd started to want a family as much as she once had with Sterling.

Only, that part of her relationship with him hadn't worked out, either, she thought as her cell phone vibrated.

She looked at the screen and frowned.

"Problem?"

"I need to go back to the hospital. Carlson Willoughby and his wife are asking to speak to me."

"WE NEED MORE information before we'll be able to say for certain what's going on," Violet told the senior couple forty-five minutes later when she joined them in Carlson's hospital room.

"But some of the results are in, aren't they?" Wanda asked, wringing her hands. Today's tracksuit was a daffodil yellow, with white racing stripes running up the sides of the pants and sleeves. "I heard some of the nurses talking…"

Violet glanced over at her patient. He looked tired and washed-out. The stress of the tests had definitely taken a toll on the eighty-two-year-old. "We're still waiting for the radiologist's report on the X-rays that were done today, but we do have the blood work."

"And?" Wanda asked.

Violet consulted the chart. "Some of the numbers—white count and calcium, for instance—are up."

"So the cancer is back." Wanda fretted, adjusting the shoulder of her husband's hospital gown.

Violet lifted a hand. "Not necessarily. There could be a lot of other reasons for that, and for the intermittent pain Carlson has been having. But I do want to cover all the bases and have an MRI and a PET scan done first thing tomorrow morning."

Carlson struggled to find the remote control for his hospital bed. "So." He plucked it out from beneath the blankets, squinted. "Then can I go home?"

"Tomorrow, after we get that done," Violet promised.

Her patient pushed the buttons—clearly trying to sit up. Instead, the back of the bed went down. He frowned in surprise as his head hit the pillow. "Why not now?"

"Because you're still feeling a little woozy from the medicines you were given during the upper and lower GI tests, and I don't want you falling or fainting again."

"Thank goodness." Wanda sighed in relief. "I can't handle him when he's not thinking clearly."

Carlson pushed the button repeatedly, obviously not understanding why he wasn't sitting up, as he clearly wished to do. "I'm thinking just fine!" he said.

Violet winked at Wanda. She walked over to the buttons on the side of the bed and helped move the older gentleman upright. "How about I order you something to eat and drink?"

He considered. "Chocolate cake?"

Wanda scolded, "That's not very nutritious. Especially for someone who hasn't had anything to eat or drink all day."

Carlson shrugged and grinned mischievously. "If I'm going to be stuck here, I may as well enjoy it." He patted the mattress beside him, lifted the arm that held the IV aside and sent his wife an openly lascivious look. "Why don't you come up here and join me and we'll have another anniversary—of sorts?"

Wanda gasped at her husband's ribald humor.

Violet chuckled and shook her head, aware it was almost dinnertime. "Let me go see what I can do." By the time she reached the hall, she heard Wanda laughing at something Carlson had said.

Violet made sure his dinner—and dessert—was on the way, then went on upstairs to the nursery. Somehow, she was not surprised to see Gavin in the recliner-rocker, little Ava in his arms.

A more natural daddy had never been made.

"Notice anything different?" he said when she approached.

Besides the fact the sight of the two of you like this takes my breath away?

Violet forced herself to be cautious. "No nasal cannula?"

"Bingo." Gavin grinned. "She's breathing just fine on her own now. Bridgette says she has been all afternoon."

"Wow." That *was* a milestone.

Bridgette appeared with a gently warmed bottle of formula and a burping cloth. "Ready to give this a try?" she asked them both.

Another milestone? Already?

Gavin stood and motioned for Violet to take his place in the chair.

As soon as she had, he handed baby Ava over.

"Violet is."

Chapter Five

Violet had never seen Gavin opt out of any medical procedure. But it was clear, from the look on his handsome face, that he was excusing himself from this.

Telling herself it came with the temporary guardianship, Violet took the bottle of gently warmed formula and pressed it against Ava's lips. The newborn's mouth turned out in a pouty frown.

"Come on now, sweetheart," Violet whispered, trying again. "You have to eat." Otherwise it would be back to taking her nutrition through a tube that went straight to her stomach via gavage feeding.

Eyes still shut, Ava pushed the bottle away with a thrust of her lower lip and replaced it with her thumb.

Violet gently eased the tiny finger out and replaced it with the nipple. Seeming not to realize it wasn't her thumb she had in her mouth, Ava sucked on the tip with just enough pressure to cause a bubble to appear in the milky liquid. Her tiny brow furrowed as she got her first taste of nutrient-rich formula. The infant paused, as if thinking about it, then suckled again, just as cautiously.

Violet and Gavin grinned. "Congratulations," Bridgette said with a wink of approval. "You win a Mommy Gold Star."

Mommy, Violet thought a little wistfully.

Aware that for the first time since Sterling had died—

and all her romantic dreams along with him—she could envision herself one day becoming a mother. When the time and the man, if there ever was another man able to take Sterling's place in her heart, was right, that was.

"It's kind of amazing, isn't it?" Gavin murmured, watching Ava continue to feed. "And such a responsibility."

Realizing the future well-being of the child in her arms rested on her and Gavin, Violet nodded. "I just hope we're able to do right by her," she whispered.

"We will," Gavin said firmly, confident as ever.

Looking into his eyes, Violet could believe it.

She and Gavin might not know a lot about taking care of a newborn infant, but they were both dependable adults and quick studies.

Together, she imagined that they could handle whatever came up, until the time came when they bundled Ava off to her permanent home.

In the meantime, they had a mission to accomplish.

A wave of affection pouring through her, Violet watched the baby's little bow-shaped lips work. Then she looked back at Gavin's sister. "How much should she take before I stop to burp her?"

"An ounce would be good," Bridgette said with the authority of a pediatric nurse before moving off to tend to another patient.

"I'm guessing you've done this before?" Gavin murmured, pulling up a chair. He watched, entranced, and Violet shared his fascination. She imagined this was how most new parents felt—completely besotted, even as they were also a bit overwhelmed with the sheer responsibility of it all.

She smiled back at him, amazed at how close she felt to him, too, in this moment. "Give a baby a bottle? Sure I've done that. But never to a child this young. And I've never given any infant their *very first* bottle-feeding."

Gavin leaned closer, his jaw brushing Violet's shoulder. He took Ava's free hand in his, her palm looking impossibly small and delicate resting against his. Grinning, he let Ava wrap her fist around his little finger and hold on tight. "She seems to like it," he observed as Ava's other hand came up to explore the bottle.

"She does at that," she said softly.

For several more minutes they watched as Violet worked to get Ava her nutrition in this new and important way. Eventually, though, the progress ceased.

Noting the infant had slowed her feeding, Violet set the bottle aside and gently shifted Ava to an upright position over her shoulder. She rubbed Ava's back until a ladylike burp escaped her parted lips. The baby sighed. Gavin and Violet both chuckled.

Noting Ava had taken only half an ounce, Violet settled her back in her arms and offered the bottle again. Ava sighed sleepily, shook her head. Violet tried again. With a yawn, Ava accepted the nipple but refused to wake enough to suckle.

Several more minutes passed.

Nothing changed.

Gavin signaled they needed assistance.

"I couldn't get her to take any more formula," Violet told Meg when she came over to help.

The nursing supervisor made a note on Ava's chart of the food consumed, then transferred the baby back to her warming bed. "This was good for the first time," she told them.

"What's the goal?" Gavin asked.

Being careful not to disturb the monitor wires taped to Ava's chest, Meg changed Ava's diaper. "We want to get her to the point she's taking in two ounces of formula by bottle every two hours, and gaining an ounce a day."

Not sure whether she was in physician or mom mode,

Violet typed the info into her phone. "What's she doing now?"

"She's been gaining half an ounce a day since she arrived at LCH. When she was first born, it was more like a quarter of an ounce. So she has a ways to go before she can be released. In the meantime," Meg advised with the experience of a mother of four and grandparent to a dozen more, "you two should head home and get as much rest as you can in anticipation of the very busy days and nights ahead."

VIOLET AND GAVIN walked out of the hospital together. They paused in front of his pickup. The bed of the truck was still covered with the tarp he had draped over their purchases in San Angelo. The backseat and cargo compartment of Violet's SUV were similarly filled with bulky bags and boxes.

"Want me to drive this stuff out to McCabe House now?" he asked.

Abruptly looking a little skittish, as if she were wondering if he intended to put the moves on her again, she hesitated. "Sure you don't want to just do it tomorrow?"

He lifted his shoulders in a lazy shrug, his need to claim her as his growing by leaps and bounds. "Why put off tomorrow what can be done today?"

She tilted her head, studying him closely from beneath her dark lashes. "You haven't had dinner."

How did she know he was hungry again? For her and food. "Neither have you," he pointed out, stepping closer.

Amusement glimmered in her eyes. "I'm not cooking for you."

"Good." He tried not to think about all the things he wanted to do to make her go weak in the knees. "'Cause I'm not cooking for you, either." He tapped her playfully on the nose. "I will stop and get a pizza for both of us en route, however."

She radiated an indifference he hoped she didn't really feel. "You wouldn't mind?"

"It's only fair." Especially if it eventually meant another chance to hold her in his arms. Maybe get in another kiss, or two, or three… "Since you paid for lunch, I'll spring for dinner."

"Okay, if you insist." She unlocked her SUV, climbed behind the wheel with a shake of her head and waited for him to close the door. When he did, she put down the window and leaned out to add, "But I can't help but think you're getting the short end of the stick here, cowboy."

A faint smile tugged at his lips. "Not to worry. I'll figure out a way to collect."

VIOLET KNEW GAVIN was only teasing, that the only way anything amorous would ever happen between them was if she wanted it to happen. Still, her mind was filled with tantalizing thoughts as she drove to McCabe House.

It was nearly seven when she arrived. The crew was gone. The container of construction debris was full. And the stable-house and landscape of the ranch was dark as could be.

Reminding herself to get some of the outdoor lights set on timer, Violet left her headlamps on, got out, opened up the stable-house and turned on the interior and exterior lights.

It felt only slightly less lonely. She went back to turn off her SUV and begin the process of unloading her purchases.

Gavin pulled up a short time later. He carried in a pizza box, a plastic container of salad and a six-pack of Texas beer. "You didn't tell me what kind of pizza to get, so I had to guess."

She cleared the wrought-iron table to make way for the food. "The suspense is killing me."

He opened the box with a flourish. "The Tex-Mex special, of course."

Made with red enchilada sauce, jack-cheddar cheese, chorizo, peppers and onions, it was indeed her absolute favorite. "Gold star for you," she murmured.

"Is the way to a woman's, ah…"

She guessed where he was going. "Heart or bed?"

He lifted his hand as if about to take the witness stand. "I'm taking the Fifth on that."

"I figured. And if you want to know the truth, *neither.*"

"Really?"

She spread her napkin across her lap. "It's men who can be enticed with a good meal."

"Exactly why you're *not* going to cook for me?"

Violet blushed despite herself. "I think I'll take the Fifth on that."

They both grinned.

Violet moved the conversation to more neutral territory. When they finished eating, she thanked him again for dinner as they cleared away the mess. Adding facetiously, "If I didn't know better, I'd think you were trying to get on my good side."

Gavin carried the trash outside to the cans. "That would imply you have a bad side."

Violet lingered in the doorway, admiring the silhouette he cast. Broad shoulders, trim waist, cute butt, long muscular legs beneath the jeans. What was not to like?

"You don't." He removed the tarp from the back of his truck.

Violet had been put in the Angel category once. Not again. "Sure I do," she vowed, matter-of-fact.

Together they carried in the boxes, then went back for more.

He slanted her a skeptical glance. "You have flaws?"

With a pensive sigh, she stacked shelving poles in the corner, out of the way. "Plenty of them."

He followed suit, dusted off his hands. "List 'em."

Trying not to notice how he towered over her whenever they stood side by side, she led the way up the steps to the Conestoga wagon. Throwing back the flap, she pointed to the stacks of clothes on her bed. "I'm hopelessly messy."

He shrugged. "I've heard of worse things."

Deciding she might as well carry some of the discarded clothing down to the sofa, she grabbed an armload. Looking not the least bit put off, Gavin followed suit.

"I really can't cook all that well," Violet continued affably. And that was something she intended to remedy now that she had a few months off ahead of her.

Another shrug. "Join the club."

She picked up two suitcases and brought those down the stairs, too. "I'm hopelessly idealistic."

Eyes narrowing, Gavin continued giving her a hand. "Yeah. I can see where that would be a problem," he allowed, more seriously now.

"Because you're cynical to a fault."

He followed her back up to her bedroom, looking casually at home once again. "Practical," he corrected, "and it's a virtue."

Violet plucked several pairs of shoes from the floor and tossed them through the opening onto the floor below. "Not if you never even *hope* for anything to work out exactly the way you wish."

He was so tall he had to bend his head to keep from hitting the canvas wagon top. Folding his arms in front of him, he theorized. "Maybe I've just learned to settle for whatever I can get and be happy with that."

"How come?" she asked, suddenly feeling self-conscious.

"Part of it probably goes back to my parents dying in that accident when I was about to start medical school."

That tragedy had reverberated throughout Laramie County and she studied the lingering sadness in his expression. "And the rest?"

"No one gets it all, Violet," he said, his tone low and rough.

"My parents have. They have a love that's endured. Six daughters. Four sons-in-law and grandchildren. Extended family. Thriving careers. A nice home." She sighed wistfully. "Four of my sisters are pretty happy now, too. And Poppy will be, once she and Trace get the family they want."

Gavin caught her hand in his, held her when she would have run. "Whereas you…?"

Tipping her head back, she took a deep breath. "Lost—" *and let down* "—the only man I ever loved."

He was silent, considering.

Gently, he stroked his thumb across the back of the hand he held. His eyes probed hers. "So you don't think you could ever love again?"

Could? It was more a question of *would.* Violet bit her lip. Not sure she wanted to risk that kind of heartache. Not sure she could go on indefinitely without romantic love, either. And still have any kind of real happiness, anyway. "I'm not sure I *want* to love again," she said finally.

Clearly not the answer the man in front of her was looking for. Leveraging his grip on her hand, Gavin pulled her against him. "Then how about just having an affair?" he asked huskily.

AN AFFAIR WAS NOT what Gavin wanted from Violet. It was also the surest way to bring her back to life. To make her admit that she was still a flesh-and-blood woman who had her whole life ahead of her. If she would only allow herself to want more.

"Gavin…" A low sound escaped her throat as his head lowered to hers.

He'd half expected her to offer some resistance, even if it was only token. And she did, going completely still at first, then slowly, inevitably lifting her arms to wreathe his shoulders and sinking against him.

"Tell me you don't enjoy kissing me." Appreciating the sweet, hot, tempting taste of her mouth, he ran a hand down her spine, bringing her so close she could feel his hardness pressing against her. Lifting his lips from hers, he strung kisses along her jaw, her ear, the nape of her neck, and felt her quiver in response. "Tell me you don't enjoy this."

She moaned at the onslaught of pleasure inundating them both. She dug her fingers into his shoulders and kissed him with a wildness beyond his most erotic dreams. "I'm human."

"Exactly." Satisfaction roaring through him, he savored the taste and feel of her. "I am, too." He pulled her closer still and went back to kissing her. Slowly and evocatively now. Until she went up on tiptoe and rocked against him, her hands sliding over his shoulders, down his back. Pressing lower, lower still.

"Okay," she said finally. Stepping back, looking slightly dazed, she sucked in an impatient breath. "Let's have a fling."

He watched her tug her shirt over her head and let it flutter to the floor. She toed off her boots. Her gaze still holding his, she worked her jeans down her thighs.

The body was no mystery for them. And hadn't been since they'd started medical school.

But damn, if she wasn't the most beautiful woman he'd ever seen. He caught her hand before she could undo the clasp of her bra. "Let me."

Her skin felt silky and warm beneath his fingers. Hot

with anticipation, he undid the clasp and eased her bra down over her arms.

Her breasts were full and round, the nipples taut and rosy. She wore cotton boy-cut panties that started just below her navel. He hooked his thumbs into either side of them and pulled them down. Past the damp curls. Over her thighs. Past her knees. He knelt to help her step out of them and then, once there, decided to stay.

Violet gasped as he wrapped his arms around the backs of her knees and buried his face in her sweet, warm softness.

Catching his head in her hands, she held on to him. Quavering now. "Gavin…"

He kissed the satiny softness. He might be doing all the work but she wasn't the only one in heaven. "Hush. I'm working here."

She laughed, shakily this time, and threaded her hands through his hair, giving him a glimpse of what it would be like if she really let go. "I thought we'd get into bed…"

And rush through this? No way. He dropped butterfly kisses. Slow, deliberate. Determined to help her find release. "In due time."

She shuddered again but did not resist.

Hands curling around the backs of her legs, he spread her thighs apart, gently guiding her until she was standing astride his denim-clad thighs, the insides of her ankles rubbing against the outsides of his legs.

"Gavin…"

"So soft." He rubbed his thumb along the feminine seam, coaxing her to let all her inhibitions float away, to open for him even more. Let himself live in the moment. "So sweet…"

Violet quivered, holding on voraciously.

Heart racing, Gavin drank in the scent and heat and feel of her. Found what he'd only fantasized about up till now, until his body pulsed and she melted against him, shuddering uncontrollably, then going hot and rigid with need.

Feeling her climax was almost his undoing.

But that was nothing compared to the feel of her hands on his shoulders, urging him upward, or her fingers undoing his belt and reaching for his fly. "It's definitely my time now," she whispered.

Gavin laughed, as Violet hoped he would.

She wanted to keep this light and easy and sexy. The best way to do that, she knew, was to concentrate on the purely physical aspect of pleasure and the hot, hard body in front of her.

"Nice," she said as she helped him off with his jeans and then his shirt. His pecs were hard, his shoulders broad. Chest covered with a nice mat of hair that arrowed to his navel and beneath the boxer-briefs. Eager to explore what was beneath, she knelt and eased off his shorts. Then as long as she was down there…

His hands clamped over her shoulders. "Not on your life." With one smooth motion, he brought her onto the bed and then stretched out beside her. "The first time we're together like this, I'm going to be inside you."

She turned, covered him with the length of her body, lowered her head and kissed him feverishly. Kissed him until everything slipped away but the feel of his big, warm body. Kissed him until those clever lips were all she wanted, all she needed.

Suddenly she was on her back again and his lips were on her breasts, savoring, drinking her in. One hand was beneath her, lifting her, the other was between her thighs. He stroked his thumb over her flesh and she was spiraling again, gone, her cry of pleasure seemingly pushing him over the edge, too.

With a grin of pure masculine satisfaction, he found his pants and the condom in his wallet.

She watched, breathlessly, as he rolled it on. And then he was over her once again, nudging her knees farther apart, sliding home. She wrapped her arms around him, opening up to him, and then there was nothing but the fusing of their bodies, the slow, sensuous, ever-deepening movement. The sensation of being taken. Possessed. Found. Until there was nothing but pleasure, nothing but the chance to feel really and truly alive once again.

THEY RETURNED TO reality with a swiftness that astounded Gavin. "Regrets?" he asked her softly when she finally untangled her body from his.

Her breath still coming quick and erratically, Violet sat up. "No. Oddly enough."

That was quite an admission from a romantic idealist like Violet, he thought. He studied the deliciously tousled state of her silky dark hair and her flushed skin, the desire to make love to her again fiercer than ever.

Sobering slightly, Violet reached for her clothes and began to dress. "I've always been hardwired to think that being in love was essential to having satisfying sex." She pivoted and looked him right in the eye. "It was a revelation to realize that's not necessarily the case." She grinned naughtily. "At least, not for the two of us."

Aware the key to this happening again was keeping the situation as casual as they both needed it to be, Gavin drawled, "Meaning you'd be willing to hook up with me again?"

"I would. If only for the stress relief. Except..." Violet paused. "I don't want things to get too complicated, and we already have the whole joint guardianship thing going on."

Which was difficult enough to manage on its own.

Sensing it would be a mistake to push her, he nodded his agreement. "You're right. We don't have to decide anything tonight." Especially if doing so would cause her to panic where the two of them were concerned.

He finished tucking in his shirt, retrieved his wallet and slid it into the back pocket of his jeans. Reluctantly, he gave her an indulgent smile. "I'm guessing this is my cue to leave."

"Actually, if you're game for it, there is something else I'd like to do."

Chapter Six

Gavin stared at Violet in surprise. "You really want to put together the closet system *tonight*?"

Unwilling to admit just how much she wanted to spend time with him, at least for a little while longer, Violet shrugged.

She opened a second beer for both of them. Their fingers brushed as she handed him the icy-cold beverage. Aware most guys couldn't wait to show off their manliness, she continued cheerfully, "With your help. If you're game?"

He studied the stack of boxes and components while he sipped.

"The hardest part will be getting everything out of the boxes and the protective wrap," Violet told him.

Aware she hadn't felt this happy and relaxed in a long time, she got out her toolbox and set it on the floor beside them. "I love putting stuff together. Don't you?"

"Ah." He rubbed at the back of his neck, as if trying to figure out how to phrase it. "Honestly? No."

Surprised to realize she didn't know as much about him as she'd previously thought, Violet found a pair of utility scissors and knelt beside a box. "How come?"

He offered a sheepish grin. "I'm really bad at it."

"Wow." She rocked back on her heels "At last, something you can't do and do well."

His gray-blue eyes sparkled with self-deprecating humor. "Which is why I usually avoid purchasing anything that requires assembly."

"Too frustrating?" Their shoulders brushed as they began taking wrapped pieces out of the box.

"And time-consuming." He lifted the heavier pieces, leaving the lighter ones for her. "Especially when you get halfway through and realize you've put a part on either backward or upside down and have to go back and disassemble everything." He inclined his head in recalled frustration. "Or you *do* finish and you have two parts left over when you should have none and you have no clue where they were supposed to go."

Violet couldn't help but laugh. "Sounds like you have had experience with this."

"However," he continued, pausing to pluck a stray piece of packing material from her shirt, "as you can see, I am good at taking things out of boxes and lining them up and handing them over for anyone who does have a knack for building things." *And making love. And making you feel like life isn't so dull and empty, after all.*

Violet winked. "Sounds like we'll make a good team, then."

And as it happened, they did.

Two hours later they had everything but a drawer system on wheels put together. "Eight down, one to go," Gavin announced.

"Except…" Violet said with a yawn as the last of her adrenaline faded and accumulated fatigue suddenly hit her with a sledgehammer force. "I really am too tired." She moved closer to him, studying the new shadows beneath his eyes. "And so are you."

"I can keep going."

Uh-uh. Taking his hand, she led him away from the last box. "At least take five."

He sat on the sofa, as directed, pulling her down beside him in the process.

She landed right next to him. Ignoring the heat radiating from his powerful body, as much as the residual desire flowing through her, she asked, "How many shifts have you been working lately?"

Too many, the weary set of his shoulders said. "I pulled six midnight-to-noon shifts in a row last week. One of the other ER doc's kids had strep throat and she wanted to be there. So I took her shifts."

"Ah. No wonder. You should be home in bed."

He flashed her the kind of look that said what he really wanted was to make love with her again. "I'll get there, eventually," he promised, pulling his phone out of his shirt pocket. He checked the screen, frowned in obvious concern.

"Everything okay there?"

Gavin exhaled roughly. "I left several messages for Nicholas and still haven't heard back from him."

"Do you think he got back to college okay?"

Gavin thumbed through his messages until he found what he was looking for. "Bridgette says he texted her at noon to say he made the trip okay but decided not to return the rental for another day or so."

"I'm guessing his vehicle is in the shop?"

"Insurance is going to cover the repairs, but it will take at least a month."

"Bummer."

"Yeah. My little brother wasn't very happy about that." Gavin looked at his phone. "He still should have called."

"He's a teenager," Violet soothed. "Maybe he's out with friends, recounting his near-death experience. Talking about it will help him get over it."

"I hope so." With a scowl of brotherly frustration, Gavin

put the phone away. He looked at the lone box remaining, then back at Violet. "Mind making me a cup of coffee?"

"No problem." Any activity was better than sitting on the sofa next to him, thinking about throwing caution to the wind and making love with him again. Aware she could really get used to having Gavin around, Violet walked over to her single-cup brewer and looked at the premeasured pods. "Light, strong or medium roast?"

Gavin slouched until his head rested against the back of the sofa and stretched his long legs out in front of him. "The closest thing to jet fuel you've got."

She chuckled. "Been there."

Rummaging around, she found a dark chocolate candy bar with fruit and nuts to go with it. When she turned around, cup in hand, she stopped at what she saw.

His eyes were shut, his arms spread wide on either side of him. And it was clear from the deep, even breathing that he had fallen fast asleep.

She set the coffee and chocolate bar on the end table and sat next to him, her knee brushing his muscular thigh.

"Hey." She shook his shoulder once, twice. He barely budged. That settled it. No way was he getting behind the wheel.

"Gavin," she said softly, "come to bed." She shook him harder and he blinked, disoriented.

"I said, come to bed. You can sleep here tonight. With me."

GAVIN WOULD HAVE thought he was dreaming, except dreams didn't carry with them the heavenly scent of Violet's hair and skin or the soft warmth of her hands rubbing his shoulder.

He tried to formulate a response, but he was so damn tired the words would not come. So when she took him by the hand and led him up the stairs into her wagon, he went unresistingly.

Nor did he resist when she sat him on the edge of the bed, knelt to help him off with his boots and then guided him back, so he could stretch out on the mattress.

He struggled to stay awake. But the moment his head hit the pillow, darkness descended.

The next thing he knew it was dawn. Still in her clothes, too, Violet was cuddled up against him, her head on his chest, her breathing soft and even.

As he wrapped his arms around her, his heart filled with a rush of unfamiliar emotion. Contentment. Peace. And a yearning so strong it scared him.

He'd gotten through the years since the tragedy that had upended his family's entire existence by not ever expecting too much out of life. He'd entered—and ended—his engagement to Penelope much the same way.

Violet made him want more.

But needing anyone—or anything—like that could be dangerous.

He'd gotten used to living day by day. Appreciating each moment as it came. Never thinking much further ahead. Upending all that could risk his hard-won serenity. With a reluctant sigh, he closed his eyes.

Patience was not—had never been—his strong suit. But if he wanted to make love to Violet again, he would have to tread very carefully.

Otherwise they both might end up regretting it.

VIOLET WOKE SHORTLY after seven in the morning. The canopy over the top of the wagon-bedroom made it difficult to see the sun streaming in through the tall windows of the stable. But she could hear the sounds of the caravan of pickups coming up the gravel lane.

Lamenting her tardiness—she had intended to be up

and out of bed well before this—she eased from the cradle of Gavin's arms and slipped soundlessly from the bed.

Tiptoeing down the stairs, she crossed the cement floor and went into the bathroom. Five minutes later order was restored to her hair. With her face washed and makeup on, a nice, minty-clean taste in her mouth, she felt a whole lot better. Although she still looked as if she had slept in her clothes.

And that was, of course, when she heard the sharp rapping on the stable-house door.

The last thing she wanted was anyone seeing Gavin in her bed! Quickly, she eased from the bathroom, stepped into her cowgirl boots on the way to the door and swung it open, expecting the construction boss to be on the other side.

Instead, it was her triplet sister Rose, a basket of goodies from her local produce business looped over her arm. Her three preschool triplet children stood beside her. Stephen had a basket of muffins. Sophia was carefully cradling a carton of farm-fresh eggs. Scarlet had a bag of freshly roasted coffee beans. "Surprise!" they said in unison. "We came to check on you!"

Looking as happy as could be, which was always the case since she had fallen in love with Clint McCulloch, Rose grinned. "We don't have a lot of time. I have to get the kids to school. But we wanted to drop by to see how you were doing. Good, from the looks of it. Although," she teased with sisterly affection, "if that's the state of all your clothes, you could use an iron."

"Ha-ha."

Behind Rose, the construction boss waved at Violet. She waved back.

One by one, the kids handed Violet their gifts. "Where do you want the rest of this?" her sister asked, hefting the wicker basket full of local jams, cheeses and plethora of fresh fruit and vegetables. "If you want, I can bring over a baker's rack, too."

"Uh, thanks," Violet said, wondering how she was going to keep Rose from realizing she had company. Out of the corner of her eye, she saw the triplets run past her. To her dismay, they were headed straight for the Conestoga wagon.

"I'm going to see the bed!"

"Me first!"

"No, me!"

Violet lifted a hand to stop them.

Rose jumped in. "Kids! That's not a toy, that's Aunt Violet's bedroom!"

Too late, the little ones had disappeared beneath the flap that served as a bedroom door. A squeal in three-part harmony sounded. All commotion abruptly stopped.

Violet briefly put a hand over her eyes.

"What's going on?" Rose demanded, seeming to realize that her triplet knew exactly what was going on.

"You're about to find out," Violet answered softly.

Sure enough, the flap opened up. "Mommy!" All three heads popped out. "Aunt Violet's got a prince sleeping in her bed!"

IT WASN'T THE first time he had been called a prince, Gavin thought as he struggled to blink himself awake. However, it was the first time he had been designated one in quite that way.

He passed a hand over his face, pushed up on his elbows and looked straight into the curious faces of three rambunctious four-year-olds. Rose McCulloch's triplets.

Scarlet pushed her glasses higher up on her nose. "He's not a prince!" she declared loudly.

"Then why is he *there*?" Sophia pointed. "If he's not waiting for some princess to come in and kiss him or something?"

Gavin couldn't help it.

He laughed.

"I'm not a prince," he said, swinging his legs over the side of the bed. "I'm a friend of your aunt's."

"Did you have a sleepover?" Stephen asked, looking a little suspicious and a lot protective.

The innate male need to protect one's territory, Gavin thought. And Violet was worth protecting. "I was too tired to drive last night. So I stayed here," he explained, getting to his feet.

"In the same bed?" Sophia and Scarlet asked in unison.

Thankfully, the flap opened. Violet stood in the wagon entry. "Okay, everybody out." She motioned for them to go.

She gave him a beseeching look as he neared, seemingly to ask him to play it cool. He quirked his lips, trying hard to keep a straight face as he followed her out onto the steps.

"Mommy, Aunt Violet had a sleepover!" Scarlet announced.

"With a prince. Only, he's not a prince," Sophia explained.

"In the same bed!" Stephen declared, folding his arms in front of him.

Rose arched a brow in her direction.

Busted, Violet thought.

"You know what?" Rose said, rounding up her children. "We're going to be late to school if we don't get a move on, so say goodbye to Aunt Violet."

"'Bye!" they shouted in unison.

"Sorry!" Rose mouthed as she shepherded her children out the door.

Before she could shut it, the construction foreman appeared in the doorway. "Hey, Doc—" he looked at Violet "—you mind coming over to McCabe House and okaying a few things for me?"

By the time Violet returned, Gavin was gone. There was a note on the coffee table.

Thanks for the hospitality last night. Sorry if I made things awkward for you with the family. See you at the hospital later. Gavin.

It was a nice note. Casual. Polite. So why did it make her feel so oddly bereft?

Violet didn't know.

She *did* acknowledge that she had no time to fret about it. Not when she needed to shower, get to the hospital to see Ava and then check to see if the rest of the test results on Carlson Willoughby had come in.

"Oh. We've just fed her and put her back in her bed," Bridgette said when Violet stopped by the Special Care Nursery.

Violet looked at the chart. "She's no longer being fed by gastric lavage?"

"She's able to take enough nutrition in on her own."

"Wow. That's great news."

"Isn't it?" Bridgette beamed. "Listen, why don't you come back again in two hours, if you can? You could handle the feeding and cuddling then. Who knows? We might even let you do the diaper change, too!"

Violet grinned. "I will."

As soon as she stepped off the elevator, she ran into the chief of oncology, Dr. Bart Remington. The tall, lanky Texan had an amazing teaching talent and a crusty demeanor that belied his soft heart. He paused, the top of his bald head shining beneath the fluorescent lights. "Our new staff oncologist, Tara Warren, is here."

Violet moved back against the wall to let an orderly pass. "I thought she wasn't going to start for a few more days."

"She's not. But she wanted a chance to go over the charts and get up to speed on the patients she'll be seeing. Since you've already treated most of them, anything you can do to assist her would be appreciated."

"I'll stop by her office as soon as I check in with radiology."

Remington patted her shoulder. "Thanks. You know, we still have room for you, at least in a part-time capacity, if you'd like to stay on, too."

Violet nodded.

"Or at least until you finish up the work you're doing for McCabe House."

Violet hesitated. She'd thought she needed to be by herself to think. Now she knew being alone might not make that easier. Instead, it might lead her to obsess about Gavin and their one reckless night together...

"Second thoughts about leaving?" the chief asked, hopeful as ever.

Second thoughts about a *lot* of things, Violet mused.

In the meantime, as she headed into the radiology department to look at films, she had responsibilities to fulfill.

Gavin was on his way to track down Violet—and to see if she wanted to take Ava's next bottle-feeding—when he heard soft sobs from Carlson Willoughby's hospital room.

Violet's voice, soothing.

More distress. From Mrs. Willoughby?

The door to the room shut softly.

Silence fell in the hall.

Gavin went on to the nurses' station. One eye on the hall, he chatted up the son of a patient who had recently come through the ER, until the door finally opened and Violet stepped out. No sooner had she cleared the portal than her composure began to crack.

He said goodbye to the son and hurried to catch up with her. "Everything okay?"

She dragged in a deep breath, nodded.

The moisture glistening in her eyes said otherwise. Hand to her elbow, Gavin steered her into a nearby supply closet and shut the door behind them.

Violet rolled her eyes. "Really?" she choked out. "What are we—sixteen?"

"We wish. What's going on?"

For a moment he thought she was still too overwrought to tell him. She ran a hand over her eyes and took another deep breath. "I had to give Carlson and Wanda Willoughby test results."

"His cancer returned?"

She nodded. Head down, she pinched the bridge of her nose. "I hate giving bad news."

He wrapped his arms around her. "Don't we all."

A shudder passed through her chest and she began to cry again.

He held her close, aware that holding her didn't change the situation. But, in that moment, he felt less alone. As her body softened and molded to his, and she slowly stopped crying, he guessed she did, too.

Another moment passed.

Neither of them spoke.

Finally, Violet blotted the tears from her face and stepped back. "I've got to go see Ava."

He brought her to him for another quick squeeze before she opened the door, then fell into step beside her. "I'll go with you."

Violet had just settled into the chair, Ava in her arms, Gavin beside her, when Mitzy Martin walked in.

The social worker looked at both of them. "We have to talk."

Chapter Seven

"If Ava continues to improve at the current rate, she is going to be released from the hospital by the end of the week. So we all need to figure out what the next step is," Mitzy said. "Do you want to put Ava with a foster family?"

"No," Gavin and Violet said in unison.

Aware they'd sounded a little too emotional, Violet promised, "We said we would care for her until a permanent placement could be found."

Gavin cast a fond look at her and the baby. "And we're going to do that," he said.

"Okay."

To Violet's relief, Mitzy did not argue with their decision. She made a note. "Where?"

This time they had no ready answer.

"And don't tell me the stable-house," Mitzy told Violet preemptively, lifting her hand. "Because your current setup is a little too primitive for a premature infant. Especially when other, better options are available."

Gavin lounged against the visiting room wall, hands shoved into the pockets of his jeans. "We could use my house."

Mitzy looked as skeptical about the idea as Violet felt.

Violet turned to Gavin. "It's awfully small, isn't it?"

Gavin shrugged as his gaze fell tenderly to the baby in her arms. "Ava won't mind. And it has all the amenities.

Washer and dryer, full kitchen, bedroom, living room and bath."

One bedroom being a fundamental flaw. Unless she wanted to become his full-time lover. Which she did not. Her emotions were far too confused as it was.

Yet the only other option was for her to move in with one of her family members. And she wasn't sure how that would work, particularly with Gavin a participant.

Especially after what had happened with Rose's triplets that very morning.

With a reluctant sigh, Violet conceded, "I suppose I could put my wagon in the backyard at Gavin's." That way, she would at least have her own bedroom.

He ran his palm across his jaw. "How would that work if it rained?"

Good point. The canvas top was not exactly weather-proof. "Ah, not sure?"

He continued to study her with his steady blue gaze as if trying to figure something out. "Besides, don't you think that's a little silly? I'm going to be working nights. You'll be at the hospital, as much as you need to, days."

Violet sat Ava up for her to burp. "Actually, the new staff oncologist is already here. So as soon as Tara Warren is up to speed, I'll be transferring all my patients to her. And then I can focus exclusively on the construction at McCabe House."

"Unless you change your mind and decide to stay," Gavin said. As their eyes met and held, Violet felt a shimmer of tension between them.

Man-woman tension.

"Is that an option?" Mitzy asked, stunned. "Would you really do that?"

No. Maybe. I'm not sure.

Doing her best to maintain a poker face, Violet shrugged. "All I can say for certain is that I've been applying and interviewing for other jobs, and plan to be in Laramie through Christmas, helping out at McCabe House. So I'll be able to help care for baby Ava until then." She paused. "And I'll still be able to be a godparent and watch over her from a distance, after that, just the way Tammy wanted."

"I'm not going anywhere. So I'll be able to be a godparent, too," Gavin interjected.

Deciding he should have a turn, Violet stood and handed him the baby.

"Well, not to worry." Mitzy gathered up her belongings. "Given how many calls we've had with people interested in adopting Ava, we'll have a place for her long before then."

Violet knew she should feel relieved about that. But somehow, she wasn't.

"So when do you want to move your stuff to my place?" Gavin asked as they left the nursery half an hour later and walked the short distance to his home.

One of a row of "shotgun houses" that had been built in the early nineties in historic downtown Laramie, Texas, the nine-hundred-square-foot abode was one-room wide. As had all the other homes on the street, Violet knew Gavin's had been completely updated and remodeled by a local builder. It sported a covered front porch, as well as a small but well-appointed dining and living room combination front room. The middle portion of the house contained a small galley kitchen and laundry closet, while the single bedroom and bath compromised the rear.

Her sister Poppy had done the interior design, in accordance with Gavin's taste. Hence, the interior walls were a light mocha brown with white trim. The dark brown wide-planked floors coordinated nicely with the man-size leather sofa and armchair, rectangular dining table and ladder-backed chairs. Built-in cabinets and shelves, painted the same white as the trim, added to the storage space.

"Hang on. I'll get you a key." Gavin walked through the kitchen and disappeared.

Giving her a relaxed grin upon his return, he pressed the key into her hand. "So, what do you think? Are we going to be able to handle this?"

Were they?

In theory, it had seemed like such a good idea.

But now that she was here, and realized how tiny his abode was, she wasn't sure. Yet what other choice did they have? They had said they would take on this responsibility. And with Ava set to be released from the hospital soon, they had to go somewhere.

"Yes. Absolutely." Violet smiled. They were adults. They could handle this. And if they made love again, it wouldn't be the end of the world.

Nor would it be if they didn't...

So why were her nipples suddenly tingling?

Gavin ambled closer. "When do you want to bring your stuff over?"

It wasn't as if she was moving in with him. "I'm not going to show up with anything more than a suitcase."

His eyes glittered with undecipherable emotion. "Famous last words."

Her cheeks heated at his teasing tone. "With six girls in the family, and parents determined to take us on family trips every chance they got, I had to learn how to pack light from a very early age."

"Sounds like a good skill to have."

"It can make life easier."

Just as being under one roof with Ava would make things easier. So how come she was suddenly nervous about it?

Ignoring the sizzling chemistry arcing between them, Violet glanced at her watch. "Well, listen, I've got to get back to the hospital to meet with Tara Warren, and I know you've got to rest before your shift tonight, so..." She hurried past him.

"Catch you later?" He walked her as far as the front door.

As he gazed down at her, Violet had the strong sense he was thinking about kissing her again.

But did not.

Which was a good thing. Kissing would lead to touching, and kissing and touching would lead to…well, she didn't need to think about that. They had made love once with wild abandon. They did not need to do it again.

Dr. Tara Warren was in her office in the hospital annex when Violet walked in. A petite redhead, she was dressed in jeans, boots and an autumn-gold camp shirt, the sleeves rolled up past her elbows.

"You must be the Violet McCabe I've heard so much about." The other oncologist held out her hand.

Violet couldn't help but note beneath her freckles the new staff physician looked a little pale.

But maybe that was due to the fairness of her skin.

Violet took the chair offered. "Here to help you transition in any way I can."

"An offer I plan to take you up on," Tara said, taking a sip of bottled water.

She picked up the stack of folders that corresponded with the list of patients she was set to see and treat.

One by one, they went over the files, until finally they reached the most pressing case in the stack. Carlson Willoughby.

"I understand he was released from the hospital early this morning," Tara said.

Violet worked to contain her concern. "He wanted to go home."

The oncologist took the X-rays and scans and put them up on the screen so they could look at them. "Against medical advice," she intoned.

Nodding, Violet pointed to the slight mass growing near

the small colon. "I think he needs surgery. Otherwise, it won't be long before he's unable to eat at all." Probably a month at most. "But Carlson is adamantly against any further treatment of any kind for his lymphoma."

Tara rummaged around in her bag and finally plucked out a half-eaten package of gingersnaps. "How does his family feel about that?" she asked, taking a small bite of one.

Violet refused the offer of a cookie with a lift of her palm. "There's only his wife, and Wanda wants him to keep fighting."

Tara looked over the rest of the test results. For the next few minutes they talked about possible courses of treatment. Some included surgical removal of the tumor in his abdomen. Others relied on chemotherapy and/or radiation to comfortably prolong the octogenarian's life.

"I was hoping you could talk to Mr. and Mrs. Willoughby about his options," Violet said.

"Be glad to." Tara crumpled up the empty cookie package. Face pale, she walked over to throw it away. "When are they coming back for the consult?"

"Tomorrow afternoon."

"The head of oncology suggested you be there with me for the first meeting to make for a smoother transition."

"Of course." It would be good to hand the case over to a physician not so emotionally involved.

Violet paused on the way out the door. "Are you feeling okay?"

The other woman nodded. "Morning sickness. Or in this case—afternoon."

Tara was pregnant? Did everyone her age have baby fever? Including, Violet wondered, maybe even her? She smiled and offered her congratulations. "When are you due?"

"February. So I'm going to work full-time till the baby's born, then cut back to half-time."

"Does the oncology chief know this?"

Tara nodded. "Dr. Remington's been frank with me on that. He is hoping you will stay on. Take the part-time position for now, and then the full-time position when I cut back." Her forehead wrinkled. "No one's mentioned it to you?"

"Not directly," Violet admitted as she opened the door to leave. "I'm aware they want me to stay, but I had no idea you were expecting."

Still feeling a little stunned by the news, Violet headed up to see Ava. To her surprise, the newborn wasn't there.

Meg Carrigan saw her looking for the bassinet. "Ava's not here anymore," she said, taking Violet's arm and leading her into the adjacent glass-walled room. "We moved her to the regular nursery, in anticipation of her going home on Friday. But she still needs to be fed and rocked and changed. So, if you're up for it...?"

One look at that sweet baby face and Violet knew she was. "I'm happy to help," she said. For as long as she could, in any way she could. Even if it meant she was risking her heart.

"Violet?" Meg said, putting down the phone half an hour later. "Your dad wants to see you in his office."

That sounded...official. Except her dad was chief of staff, not chief of oncology. "Now?"

Meg nodded. "He said he'd like to talk with you before you head home."

Reluctantly, Violet handed Ava to Meg and headed for the business wing of the hospital. To her surprise, her mother was there, too. Both looked extremely serious.

"What's up?" Violet took a chair.

Lacey McCabe wasted no time in getting to the point. "We heard about the plan to take care of Ava in Gavin's home and we wanted to let you know there are other options."

Resentment swept through Violet. "I've already been

told by social services that my glamping arrangement is not suitable for a newborn."

Which, Violet realized belatedly, her pediatrician mom would have known from the get-go.

"You could stay with your father and me," Lacey said encouragingly. "Since you and your sisters are all gone, there is plenty of space."

Her parents *did* have a big Victorian home in town. Six bedrooms, seven baths. Five thousand square feet of room spread out over three stories.

There was only one problem. "I don't think Gavin would be comfortable there."

"Gavin could stay in his own home and visit Ava whenever he wanted," her father intoned.

Had Rose—or her triplets—been talking?

Did it matter?

Expecting her parents to respect her privacy, the way they always had in the past, Violet said tightly, "I'm not sure he'd like that, either."

Her mother tried again, even more gently. "It's just for the short-term."

Or longer. And even if it wasn't… Violet dug in her heels all the more. "It's until we find a forever family for Ava, and I'm not sure how long that's going to take."

Her father took off his glasses and rubbed the bridge of his nose. "Mitzy thought it could be accomplished in just a few weeks."

Personally, Violet thought it was going to take a lot longer to find the perfect fit for the orphaned little girl. But for the moment she let that slide. She rose gracefully. "Thanks, but Gavin and I have already worked this out."

Jackson gave his daughter a look that let her know the conversation was far from over. "We're not questioning his chivalry or his hospitality," he said.

Violet folded her arms in front of her. She hadn't felt

this called-to-task since high school. "Then what *are* you questioning?" she asked in the same blunt tone.

Her parents exchanged concerned looks. Eventually, her mother took the lead. "As I mentioned already, babies make things complicated. It's so easy to get emotionally attached. And when you're sharing that experience closely with someone of the opposite sex who you're already physically attracted to—"

"I never said that!"

"You didn't have to," Jackson grumbled.

Lacey continued to placate, as only her mother could. "It's easy to mistake the wonder and joy of new life for something else entirely."

"Bottom line," her father said, "we will fully support you if you decide you want to adopt this baby and raise her as your own."

Well, that was good to know. Not that she was planning on doing that, Violet thought with a heavy heart.

"We just don't want to see you get hurt," her dad continued. "So if you don't want to live in a place that will keep you grounded in the reality of the situation and simultaneously put the brakes on for you while you take care of this baby, then we think you should reconsider the whole arrangement."

"CAN YOU BELIEVE IT?" Violet fumed as she paced back and forth on Gavin's front porch, more furious than he had ever seen her. "My parents want us to put Ava in foster care!"

Still groggy from the pre-midnight-shift-nap he'd been taking, Gavin took Violet by the arm and pulled her into his home.

This was definitely not a discussion he wanted to have in front of his neighbors. Most of which were home, and thanks to the small acreage of their yards, within easy earshot on this beautiful fall evening.

Gavin shut the door behind them. Peering down at her, he took in the tousled state of her chocolate-brown hair, and the flush in her cheeks. "When did they say this to you?"

"Around seven-thirty."

Or in other words, an hour ago, Gavin thought, glancing at his watch. "What brought this on?"

"I don't know."

He figured she did. So he simply stood there and waited her out.

Finally, she threw up her arms and began to pace the length of his small living area. "I think they've gotten the idea, from the amount of time we've spent in the nursery, that you and I are becoming too close to Ava."

He tore his eyes from the flattering dark denim dress she'd worn to work. It buttoned all the way down the front, tied at the waist and hugged her curves in all the right places. A pair of burgundy boots completed the outfit.

He doubted they would be in anywhere near this much trouble if they weren't attracted to each other. And hadn't acted on it.

"They may have a point about that." Although he didn't regret making love to her, he conceded the timing was not the best.

She took a step closer, looking more beautiful and impassioned than ever before. "You're siding with them?" she asked in astonishment, slipping the big leather shoulder bag off her arm and tossing it on the chair. Slender hands propped on her hips, she glared at him and waited for him to respond.

Gavin sighed. The last thing they needed to do was to fight each other. He lifted a conciliatory hand. "I'm just saying that we have been put in a very unique situation. It's hard not to feel for her." *And each other...*

Especially with his body tightening this way.

"That's why we should keep Ava with us until we find a forever home for her," Violet argued softly. "To do otherwise would mean moving her from our care to that of foster parents and then to a third home after that." The corners of her lips turned downward. "That's too much for a baby who never even got to know her birth mother!"

Put like that...

Gavin walked into the kitchen and poured himself a tall glass of water from the tap, then moved away. "You have a point."

Violet lounged against the sink, her hands clasped in front of her. She glanced up at him, her expression pleading. "So you agree with me?"

"That we should remain co-guardians and not put Ava in foster care? Yes."

She released a quavering breath.

Although he could see she was relieved, he could tell by the way she was acting he hadn't yet heard the full story. He finished his glass of water and reached behind her to pour another. "What else did your parents say?"

She watched him over one shoulder. "Nothing."

Right. Except she wouldn't quite meet his gaze. Which meant it was *definitely* something.

"Does it involve me?" he persisted.

She stared straight ahead. "It's foolish."

He put the glass down and moved so she had no choice but to look him in the eye. He braced his hands on either side of her. Close enough to smell her freesia perfume. Unable to help himself, he reached out to touch her cheek. As he felt the softness of her skin once again, another jolt of desire roared through him. "And yet you're incredibly upset."

She leaned into his touch for one millisecond before pulling away. Her teeth raked across her lower lip. "Because they're so far off the mark." Averting her gaze, she eased out of his reach.

Ignoring his instinct, which was to pull Violet back into his arms and hold her until her distress subsided, he followed her into the living room. "Are they worried about you and Ava staying here with me?" He studied her closely. "Are they worried that something will happen between us?"

"We didn't go there. Exactly. But they were clearly thinking in that direction."

He caught her hand in his and this time he didn't let her go. "Because?"

"They've noticed I'm attracted to you. And I have the feeling they sense the attraction might be mutual. They also think I might be more comfortable in their home. Although they invited you to bunk there, too."

He snorted. "Ah, no."

She laughed despite herself, shaking her head in silent remonstration. "That's what I said. And for the record? Since you and I are both charged with caring for Ava— together—I still plan on staying here."

He stroked a hand through the silky softness of her hair, tucking a strand behind her ear. "Even though your parents don't approve?"

"I'm a *grown* woman," she reminded him indignantly.

He let his hand fall. "Who's now blushing bright red."

She stepped back. "Because I'm ticked off that they would even *suggest* that you and I might mistake our duty to Ava for something else," she huffed, gathering steam yet again.

He grinned at the realization that he wasn't the only one thinking about traveling that particular road.

"Like what?"

"I—I don't know."

Yeah, she did. So did he.

And it was time they both accepted and acted on that.

Leaning forward, he took her face in his hands. "Something like this?"

Chapter Eight

Violet had known Gavin would eventually kiss her again. Just as she knew that when he did, she would throw her reservations aside and kiss him back.

Nonetheless, she hadn't expected to feel a lightning bolt of passion the second their lips touched. Hadn't known she would let out an involuntary moan or curl against him quite so readily.

But she did, and her response was all the encouragement he required. He ran his hands through her hair, tilting her face up to his, and tenderly meshed his lips with hers.

Emotion poured through her.

She had never felt such incredible need.

Never wanted someone so completely.

Or felt quite as wanted in return.

Gavin lifted his head, said gruffly, "You better go if you don't want me to take you to bed."

She laughed shakily. "Leaving is not an option."

"Exactly what I hoped you would say." He tucked an arm beneath her knees and lifted her against his broad chest. Cradling her close, he carried her through the kitchen and into the bedroom.

There was barely room for anything except his king-size bed, but that was fine with her. Still kissing him, she toed off her boots and reached for the buttons on her dress. He caught her around the waist, pulling her snug against him, one of his knees riding erotically between her thighs. "Let me."

He kissed her again, one hand moving to the sash at her waist. When that was loose, he proceeded to undo the buttons. From the waist up, from the waist down, kissing her all the while.

He stopped to part the edges of her dark denim dress and grinned when he saw the red camisole and matching panties beneath. And then those were coming off, too.

The next thing she knew he was dropping her onto the bed. Following her down.

Laughing softly, she rolled so she was on top.

He rolled so she was beneath.

"I want you naked, too."

He smirked, put his mouth over hers and took her in. "We're getting there," he said, kissing her with soul-shattering finesse.

But not, apparently, until he was ready.

He nipped at her lower lip. Slid his hands beneath her and lifted her into the hard planes of his body. She rubbed against the erection straining through his pants. A whimper of need escaped her.

He caught her wrists in one hand and anchored them above her head. "More?"

"Yes."

She quivered as his mouth found her breasts, his fingertips probing the velvety warmth between her thighs.

She was wet, waiting, wanting.

Gavin couldn't get enough of her.

The softness of her skin, the way she at first surrendered, then commandeered their kiss. He could feel her fighting the want and need, and he could feel her losing the battle. She was wild in a way he could never have imagined, as giving as he could have wished. He stopped long enough to undress, grab a condom, and joined her on the bed.

She moaned low in her throat, deliciously ravaged.

He penetrated her slowly and she closed around him like a hot, wet sheath.

"Deeper?" he whispered, his palms moving across her slender thighs to her abdomen. He pressed her into the bed.

She arched as he plunged into the sweetest, silkiest part of her. "Yes," she gasped, opening up to him even more.

Wrapping her arms and legs around him, she kissed him as they moved together. And then there was no more thinking, nothing but feeling. Of passion and heat, acceptance and surrender. Nothing but this moment in time. As they shuddered together in release, and then still clinging, came slowly back to earth, Gavin knew, nothing had ever felt so right.

"You know, I hate to say it, but your timing leaves a lot to be desired," Gavin murmured.

Violet smiled at the sexy-rough voice in her ear. Her body still trembling with aftershocks, she rested her head on his chest.

He swept a hand down her spine. Sighed. Kissed her again, sending sparks down every nerve ending. "I have to be at work in an hour. So as much as I would love to spend the entire night in bed with you, I've got to hit the shower. Of course, if you're up for it, you could always join me."

"Really," she chided with a teasing grin.

"Really," he said with absolute sincerity.

And that was how they ended up making love again, albeit more quickly this time, before he finally did finish his shower and pull on a pair of scrubs.

Violet sat, wrapped in a towel, watching him dress.

Damn, but he was gorgeous.

And this was fun and wonderful.

And who cared if she didn't know quite what it was, except not a one-night stand.

He came to her, rubbed his thumb beneath her eyes. "You look tired."

She was exhausted. Physically and emotionally and every other way. Wearily she stood. "Isn't that my line?"

"Given that it's almost midnight, why don't you stay here tonight?" He reached into his closet and pulled out a button-down shirt. "I'll even let you wear this."

The idea of sleeping in his bed, in nothing but his shirt, was incredibly erotic. She studied him. "You sure you won't mind?"

He shrugged. "You're going to be sleeping here in another day or two, anyway. Wouldn't hurt to get used to the place."

To him?

Violet released a quavering breath. "Okay, Doc, you've convinced me." She really was too exhausted to drive all the way out to McCabe House, anyway.

Gavin kissed her again, then slowly, reluctantly, released her. "Make yourself at home."

"Will do," Violet promised as he headed off to the hospital.

She sank back down into the bedcovers.

The next thing she knew, it was almost noon and her cell phone was ringing.

Stunned to find she had slept so long, she answered it.

"Hey, where are you?" Poppy asked.

Violet rubbed her eyes. "Gavin's place."

"I thought baby Ava wasn't due to be released for another couple of days."

"She's not."

An interested silence commenced.

"Long story."

"O-kay." Poppy inhaled a breath. "Well, don't go anywhere, okay? Rose and Lily and I have a surprise for you."

Poppy hung up before Violet could protest.

Knowing there was no dissuading her siblings when they were on a mission, Violet sprang into action. She gathered up her clothes and dressed hurriedly. She'd barely run a brush through her hair when the doorbell rang.

Poppy, Rose and Lily stood on the other side, along with an old-fashioned baby buggy with a canopy top, a box of infant clothes and linens, a plastic baby bathtub, a car seat for newborns and a bassinet. All items that had been used by her sisters when their children were infants.

"We heard you and Gavin were going to bring Ava here for a little while, so we figured we'd all help you get set up."

"We're really going to need all this?" Violet asked, looking past them to see they had also brought a gift set from the local baby boutique that included baby bottles and a warmer, several boxes of disposable diapers and a gift pack of baby toiletries.

Poppy looked at the other two and, irrepressible as ever, said, "I told you they were a couple."

"Temporary co-guardians," Violet corrected as she helped lug everything inside.

Poppy grinned. "Uh-huh. Then why were you spending the night here when baby Ava's still in the hospital?"

"Gavin was—is working."

"Not till midnight, he wasn't. What were you all doing before that?"

Violet had no quick answer, since she wasn't about to reveal what had really been going on.

Poppy high-fived Lily and Rose. "Thought so!"

Rose sympathized. "Well, where would you expect her to go after the talk Mom and Dad gave her?"

Violet shut the door behind them. "You heard about that?"

Lily nodded. "We might have been asked to talk some sense into you. Convince you to stay at Mom and Dad's during the guardianship period."

Disappointment spiraled through Violet. "Is that why you're here?" Because her sibs thought she was making a huge mistake, too?

"Depends," Rose said cautiously, her sisterly concern evident. "Are you and Gavin an item?"

Were they a *couple*?

Violet was trying to figure out how to answer that when the front door opened and closed again.

Gavin walked in, looking hunky and handsome in hospital scrubs. He nodded at her sisters politely, then looked at Violet in concern. "Are you okay? Bridgette said you were supposed to come in this morning to feed Ava and you never showed."

Maybe she didn't have the mothering gene, after all. "I overslept," Violet admitted guiltily. The look in his eyes said he knew why. "Is everything okay with her?" she asked, suddenly anxious.

He nodded, his gaze lingering on her in a way that said she had nothing to feel bad about. "I checked on her a couple of times during the night and managed to get in a cuddle or two, and again before I left. Although I have to tell you, I pretty much had to stand in line. Little Ava's quite the darling of the nursery. All the nurses, including my sister Bridgette, are totally in love with her."

Violet understood why. The infant had suffered such a tragic loss, it was impossible not to feel for her and her late mother. Impossible not to want to snuggle her endlessly. "How is she doing otherwise?"

"Great. She's gained another half ounce since yesterday."

Unable to help but feel as though she was missing out, Violet glanced at the clock. "When's her next feeding?"

"Nurses said one o'clock or thereabouts. They're still having to wake her up instead of the other way around, but they said it won't be long before she starts clamoring for her bottle at feeding time. And then, watch out." He smiled affectionately.

For someone who had no plans to permanently care for little Ava, he certainly was emotionally involved. As was she.

Violet pushed the pang of worry aside.

Gavin looked at the plethora of baby things and the posse of McCabe females.

"Poppy, Rose, Lily…" He offered belated individual greetings to their guests with a tip of an imaginary hat. "I assume you're responsible for all the baby paraphernalia?"

Her sisters nodded proudly in unison.

Then Poppy gestured at Violet. "And we assume *you* are responsible for the new spring in our sister's step."

Violet choked. "Poppy!"

Gavin hooked an arm around her waist and tugged her against him. Kissing her temple, he grinned with masculine satisfaction. "You bet I'll take credit for that."

"WHY DID YOU imply we had something going on?" Violet demanded the moment her sisters had all left.

"Because we do." His eyes darkened as he took her in his arms. "I'm not going to hide how I feel about you, Violet."

She splayed her hands across his chest to prevent him from really kissing her this time. "And how exactly is that?"

Was he saying he wanted to start a relationship with her that went beyond their co-guardianship of Ava? And if so, how did she feel about that?

To her surprise, she felt none of the guilt she had always expected to experience when she became involved with someone other than her late fiancé.

She did feel fear, however. She didn't want to open up her heart only to be hurt all over again. And her family was right about one thing: this was definitely the kind of complex, emotional situation that could lead to just that.

The usually cynical Gavin, on the other hand, seemed to feel no trepidation. Hauling her closer, he tipped her head up. "I'm not sure I can find the words that accurately describe how I feel."

"Try."

"Okay. I'm interested in you." He smiled. "*Very* interested." Another kiss. "I want to keep on seeing you until we see where this takes us."

In an effort to inject some levity into the situation, Violet quipped, "Heartbreak City?"

He took both her hands in his. "Now who's not being honest?" he chided, practical as ever.

Violet tamped down the fantasies their two lovemaking sessions had inspired. She eased away and began stacking the baby things into a neat pile against the wall. "My parents said the joint responsibility for Ava would bring us together in ways that could be very short-lived."

And when they'd been saying it to her, she hadn't wanted to believe it. But now? Now she knew if she were smart she would not allow herself to go there. Because this all felt a little too real.

He helped her tidy up. "Then I say enjoy it while it lasts. Although for the record—" he caught her wrist and tugged her temptingly close once again "—I don't think what I'm feeling for you is a fleeting attraction." Framing her face with his hands, he lowered his head until they were nose to nose. "I think it's been simmering for a very long time."

He shifted so they were lip to lip. The closeness turned into a scorching, sensual kiss that rocked her to the core.

"Put on the back burner because of your grief over your loss," he said, kissing her again, even more ardently this time.

Finally, he lifted his head. "The fact you had some stuff to work through…"

And now that she had…

It was time to think about the future.

What she wanted, needed, had to have.

Violet took a bracing breath. For all their sakes—especially Ava's—she had to put her usual idealistic notions aside and be realistic here. "You can understand if I think you're a bad risk, then, for anything long-term or really meaningful, too. Given your own inability to forge a lasting relationship with any woman since your engagement to Penelope ended?"

GAVIN SHOULD HAVE KNOWN Violet would bring this up again at some point. He knew he had a reputation among the local ladies. "I'm not as much of a love-'em-and-leave-'em guy as the rumors would suggest," he said drily.

Beginning to drag from the night spent on duty, he went into the kitchen to put on a pot of coffee.

"But you have had several casual dating relationships in the past four years that ultimately crashed and burned."

"Three. But who's counting?"

"Any particular reason why?"

He could see she was looking for any excuse not to put her heart on the line again. Yet, for practical reasons, he couldn't sugarcoat his own deficiencies. "Sheryl—the physical therapist—thought I was too much of an enigma for my own good."

Her elegant brows knit together. She was wearing the denim dress and boots she'd had on the day before. He wasn't sure if he preferred her in that—undoing all those buttons had been fun—or in nothing but one of his shirts.

The truth was, he liked her in anything or nothing at all. Just so long as she was here.

Violet gave him a curious look. "Did you want to be a mystery?"

He sat and pulled her onto his lap. "No. I just don't like sitting around dissecting everything to the nth degree."

His not-too-subtle hint fell on deaf ears.

"What happened with Helen Shinsky?"

So she had kept up on his love life. Even though that particular part of it had occurred mostly in Kerrville, Texas, where the ER physician had worked. Trying not to feel too flattered, he revealed, "She didn't see me having what it took to ever settle down. So she ended it. Last I heard, she'd found The One and was happily married."

"And Norah?" Violet persisted.

The wedding planner. "She wanted a soul mate. I wasn't it."

"So the common theme in all the breakups was…?"

"They could get only 'so close to me' and no closer."

Which was, he thought, a shame to find they'd all felt that way. All three of the women had had everything he'd been looking for, at least from a subjective angle. Plus, at least he'd been satisfied with the way things had been. It had sucked to find out they hadn't been.

"Were you trying to keep them at arm's length?"

"No."

"Then how come they all felt excluded or shut out in some way?"

Hell if he knew. He'd tried to be forthcoming. Kind. Responsible. He exhaled, aware this was why he sometimes felt so cynical. "I think the common theme was that I didn't have a romantic bone in my body. Or in other words, I was practical to a fault."

Violet did not look surprised. He studied her expression, in tune enough with her emotions to see that an enormous red flag had been thrown up. And that did bother him, a lot. "Why do my past failures worry you so much?"

She eased off his lap and walked over to examine the gifts her sisters had brought in. Her gaze averted, she pulled out a stack of white, yellow and blue onesies, and started to sort and fold them all by color. "I just think I ought to know what to expect before I become just another on the string of broken hearts left in your wake."

This was usually the place where he became really frustrated and called a halt to the conversation, the woman and the relationship.

But not this time.

He didn't want to lose whatever this was that he had with Violet the same way. So if that meant opening up, a little bit, so be it. He walked over to where she was standing, took her hand in his and turned it palm up.

"It's not that I don't want to have the kind of deep, loving marriage that my parents had. Or my sister Erin has with her second husband, Mac Wheeler. It's just that I don't seem to have a talent for becoming really close to people, the way you obviously do." He sighed. "I mean, I've got a lot of casual friends I care about, who also care about me. Family..."

"But no one you could really bare your soul to."

He traced her lifeline with his index finger, admitting, "Not since..."

"Your parents died in that car accident the year we both started med school," she finished when he found himself unable to go on.

Her intuitiveness rendered him speechless. She put the baby clothing aside and shifted closer. She laced her slender fingers through his consolingly. "I remember how traumatic that was for your entire family."

Even though, he recalled, she'd been living in Houston at the time and he'd been in Galveston.

Ignoring the lump in his throat, he nodded, acknowledging that it had been one of the roughest times the Monroe clan had ever had. It was also the first time he'd let those closest to him down. But, sadly, not the last.

"I remember Erin had three little kids of her own. And a geologist husband who was almost never around."

Gavin exhaled, reflecting, too, on his sister's grit. "Yet Erin insisted I stay in med school while she remained in Laramie, taking care of our three younger siblings, the ranch and the Western wear store in town."

"You felt guilty?"

He closed his eyes against the crushing weight of it. "And grief-stricken." He rubbed the bridge of his nose.

"As if you were still functioning yet strangely detached?"

"Yeah, that, too."

A commiserating silence fell. "I felt numb after Sterling died, too."

Strange, that even then they'd been on parallel tracks, he thought. "How long did yours last?"

"Until just recently," Violet admitted softly.

Again, it had been the same for him.

He'd sort of sleepwalked through his previous relationships, including his engagement to Penelope. Only in the past few weeks had he begun to think that maybe he could have more than work and fun, extended family, friends.

He stared down at her, admiring her grit. "You always seemed so strong."

"Because I had a mission."

Given to her by the death of her fiancé. "Becoming an oncologist."

"The harder I worked, the better I felt," she admitted with customary idealism.

"Same here. Although when it came to my family, I always wished I could have done more."

Encouraged to go on by the understanding reflected in her gaze, he explained, "Which is why I elected to come back to Laramie for my residency. So I could be close enough to help out more. Although, once Erin married Mac and my sibs all left for college, I wasn't nearly as needed."

"So you moved into your own place and started dating."

He grimaced. "Badly, according to my reviews."

"Don't beat yourself up. That's more than I did. I've yet to actually go out on a date with anyone since Sterling died."

"But you're thinking about it."

"In the abstract maybe." Violet raked her teeth across her lower lip. "But the real question is…where do you and I go from here?"

Although not normally one to put a label on things, Gavin saw the rationale for spelling things out in this circumstance. Especially if it made Violet feel better. "We're co-guardians—temporarily," he said.

"Check."

"Friends."

"Also check!" she affirmed with a smile.

He lifted her hand to his lips and pressed a kiss into the silky-soft center of her palm. "Lovers."

There was the briefest hesitation in her eyes. A catch in her breath. "As in…exclusive?"

Wanting absolutely no doubt about that, he brought her all the way against him. "You're damn right we're exclusive."

She moved out of the circle of his arms and stood. "That sounds good to me. As long as you understand that the 'living together' part is only for as long as we have Ava. As soon as she's placed with her adoptive family, you and I will go back to our separate spaces."

"But still remain lovers and friends." He wanted to go on the record about that, too.

She nodded. "At least until I leave for a new job and the next chapter of my life, anyway."

Then, he could see she was thinking, they would have to see. Luckily, he had plenty of time to convince her otherwise.

THE DOORBELL RANG just as Gavin was about to hit the sack and Violet was readying to go to the hospital to see Ava. She turned to him. "Expecting someone?"

He shook his head.

But then, she thought as he opened the door, they hadn't been expecting her sisters to pay them a visit earlier that day, either.

Gavin stared at his little brother in shock. "What are you doing here?" His brow furrowed. "Why aren't you at school?"

Nicholas shrugged as he stepped inside. "I dropped out."

Gavin glared. "Tell me you're kidding."

He wasn't.

Thinking the two men might need a peacekeeper, Violet stayed where she was.

"The accident made me see I'm wasting my time going to college," Nicholas told his brother. "So I talked to the dean. I told him that for financial reasons related to the wreck I had to withdraw and needed at least a partial refund on my tuition and room and board for this semester. And I got it."

Gavin's scowl deepened. "They let you quit, just like that?"

Nicholas flushed. "Well, the dean said I couldn't come back unless I reapplied and was admitted to the university again, and that because of my doing this, the odds would be stacked against me. But that's okay, because I don't really want to go back."

Gavin looked at Nicholas as though he couldn't believe how lame his brother was being. He looked at Violet. "Help me out here. Explain to him why you never, ever, make important life decisions in the wake of a traumatic accident. And why it was even more stupid of him to drop out of school on a whim."

I am not the person you should be asking this.

Nicholas squinted at Violet, seeming to remember what Gavin clearly did not. "Didn't you drop out of med school or something at one point?"

Violet kept her expression inscrutable. "When my fiancé was diagnosed with cancer. Yes, I did."

Nicholas brightened, apparently thinking he'd found a kindred soul. "Do you regret it?"

"No, but…" Violet felt as though she was walking the plank here. "Our situations were different."

"And maybe they weren't," Nicholas said with a "So there!" look aimed at Gavin.

Gavin's expression looked as if it had been carved in granite. Apparently irritated she'd been no help, he turned back to his brother, demanded impatiently, "So what's the plan?"

Nicholas straightened. "I've already invested all the money I got back in the stock market."

Gavin groaned.

"Now all I have to do is go back to living at the ranch, with Mac and Erin and the kids, and working at the store, until the profits start rolling in."

Gavin's gaze narrowed all the more. "What did Erin say about this?"

Nicholas hesitated. "I thought they'd support my plan, since both Mac and Erin are really savvy business people, but they don't, so…I was hoping maybe you'd talk to them on my behalf, get them to stop being so disappointed in me."

Gavin shook his head. "Sorry, bud. I agree with them."

"I should have figured as much," Nicholas muttered. "Thanks for nothing." He spun around and headed out the door.

An uncomfortable silence fell.

Violet released the breath she'd been holding. "You were a little hard on him, don't you think?"

"I'm not going to sugarcoat the situation. He's making a huge mistake."

And so are you. "Yes, but it's done now," she said evenly.

Gavin took off his scrub shirt and the T-shirt under it in one fell swoop. "All the more reason my little brother needs to keep thinking about it, until he realizes the enormity of what he's done." He stalked toward the bedroom.

"And maybe," Violet said, following him as far as the open bathroom door, "he's not the only one who should do some soul-searching."

"You saying I'm in the wrong?" He turned the shower on and she spun around before she could see his pants come off, too.

"I'm saying it wouldn't hurt you to have a little heart."

Chapter Nine

Eight hours later Violet was in the baby boutique on Main Street, trying to find a going-home-from-the-hospital outfit for Ava, when she sensed someone coming up behind her.

She turned. Gavin stood in front of her.

Her heart skipped a beat as she let her gaze rove over his freshly shaved face and damp, sexy hair. *He sure cleans up well*, she thought wistfully. Then catching herself, bit her lip. So much for trying to act as though he had no impact on her. Glad there was only the store clerk here to observe any of this, and she was on the other side of the store, Violet settled one hand on her hip. "What are you doing here?"

"Bridgette told me where to find you."

So, he'd been to the hospital nursery, too.

Violet sighed. "I'll have to talk to her."

He cut her off before she could go to the next table of layette items. "I'm sorry." He looked at her for a long moment. "I shouldn't have dragged you into our family squabbles."

The spacious store interior suddenly felt a lot smaller. "It's Nicholas you should be apologizing to."

"Already did." He stuffed his hands into the pockets of his jeans. "You're right—it's his life to live, his mistakes to make."

Violet rolled her eyes. "I hope you didn't put it like *that*."

"I said the first and left off the last. Although it was implied." He grinned.

Violet muttered in exasperation under her breath and moved to the next display. Most of the special outfits were white. She wanted pink.

Gavin moved with her. "Bridgette also said she thought you were upset when you left the hospital."

He was standing so close they were practically touching. Violet shut her eyes. "Now I'm really going to have to talk to her."

When she opened them again, the clerk was disappearing into the stock room.

Gavin turned to lounge against the table, facing her. "Ava's doing okay…" he continued speculatively.

Tenderness rolled through Violet at the memory of the infant's last feeding, which had happened less than an hour ago. "Ava's doing *great*," she corrected.

Gavin reached up and tucked a strand of hair behind her ear. "And I'm guessing by the fact you haven't told me to get lost yet that your low mood is not about me."

It wasn't. Even though they'd had their first tiff as lovers, she had forgiven him almost as soon as the words were out. She just hadn't gotten around to making up with him. Mostly because she thought at least a little time away from each other might give her some much-needed perspective.

"So…?" he prompted.

Violet bit her lip. She had to confide in someone. And since Gavin was also a physician of record on the case… "I had that patient consult with Tara Warren this afternoon."

His look said he knew very well which one. "Didn't go well?"

Violet shook her head. "The Willoughbys are still reeling from the diagnosis," she said quietly, her heart breaking for both of them. "Not surprisingly, they didn't like any of the options presented to them." And had gone home, with Wanda still crying, Carlson completely demoralized, to think about it.

"I'm sorry to hear that."

"You and me both." Violet cleared her throat. "Anyway, I knew the boutique was open until nine this evening, and I thought it might be a good time to get something for Ava to wear when we take her home."

Gavin's brow lifted. "I thought your sisters brought us a ton of newborn clothes."

"This is a special day for Ava. It should be commemorated in some way. I didn't expect you to understand."

"Because I'm a man?" He tilted his head to one side, ribbing her with his gaze. "Or because I don't seem to have a romantic bone in my body?"

Actually, he did. He just didn't realize it yet. "Ha-ha," she retorted, aware the mischievous sparkle in his eyes had brought a telltale heat to her face. Determined not to give the returning clerk anything to gossip about, she asked cantankerously, "Now, do you want to help me with this task or not?"

He turned and selected the very outfit she'd had her eye on since she'd entered the store. "Oh, I'll help," he vowed, leaning down to whisper in her ear. "With this and anything else you might need."

That, Violet thought, was what she had been afraid of all along.

"So. How do you want to do this?" Violet asked several days later when the Big Day had finally arrived.

Bridgette stepped forward, discharge papers in hand. "Well, one of you has to ride in the wheelchair while you hold Ava. It's the rule. Because if you were carrying her in your arms and one of you tripped on the way out the door…"

"Liability issues?" Violet said.

"And an ER visit," Gavin quipped, "for one, if not both, given a parent's propensity for twisting themselves into all sorts of shapes to protect their young from harm."

Except she wasn't a parent, Violet thought wistfully. Nor was he. They were guardians and temporary ones at that.

"I think Gavin should sit in the wheelchair," she said. "Since I'm going to be the one driving us all back to his place."

Bridgette quirked a brow.

"We only had one car seat. We decided to put it in my SUV, since I'm the one not currently working full-time."

"You could always borrow another safety seat," the pediatric nurse said. "Then you'd both have one."

Gavin shook his head. "She's not going to be with us that long, sis."

"Social services hopes to find a place for her within the month," Violet added.

"If you-all don't change your minds," Bridgette said with all the impertinence of a little sister.

"We're not going to change our minds," Gavin and Violet said in perfect unison.

Bridgette gave Ava one last cuddle. "Famous last words," she said softly, smiling down at Ava. "I mean, look at her. Have you ever seen a cuter, more adorable baby girl?"

No, they hadn't, Violet thought wistfully. But thus far it appeared she was the only one who had developed a raging case of baby fever. And that being the case, there was no choice but to stick to the original plan.

While she struggled to curtail her feelings, Gavin got reluctantly into the wheelchair. Baby Ava—who was bundled up against the cool morning in her adorable pale pink onesie, knit sweater, cap and matching blanket—was handed to him. Before they were halfway down the hall, some of their colleagues appeared to cheer their exit.

Gavin mugged comically at all the attention.

Violet grinned and laughed. Like Gavin, she was happy and relieved the newborn was finally well enough to be released from the hospital.

She was also envious.

In another lifetime it might have been her sitting in that wheelchair, en route home, with her newborn in her arms, a loving husband beside her.

In another lifetime all her dreams might have come true, the way they had for four of her sisters.

Instead, she was on the verge of falling irrevocably in love with a little girl she couldn't keep, and equally in lust with a man who was every bit as pragmatic as she was idealistic.

He was okay with having only half of what he wanted.

Whereas she, Violet knew, never would be.

ALTHOUGH SHE'D BEEN briefly awake and looking around as they put her into the safety seat, Ava was sound asleep when they arrived at Gavin's home.

Carefully, he lifted the baby carrier out of the vehicle and carried it into the house, where disorganized stacks of baby things still awaited them.

Violet had meant to organize this morning, getting everything ready while Gavin was on duty at the hospital. Instead, she'd gotten caught up in a renovation emergency at McCabe House. The teardown of one wall had revealed a long-existing leak in one of the pipes. A plumber had been called, the damage assessed, and the emergency repairs approved by both her and the board of directors. By then, it had been almost noon and she'd had to rush to the hospital for Ava's release, which had been timed to occur as soon as Gavin's shift ended.

Now, here they were with Gavin looking dead on his

feet, and no place to put the sleeping infant. He said, "Where should we start?"

Violet took the carrier from him and set it in the middle of the dining table. With Ava still strapped in, she was safe and cozy for now. Turning back to Gavin, Violet touched his arm gently. "I can handle it. Why don't you go on to bed?"

Gavin shoved a hand through his hair. "You sure?"

Yes, she was sure. If he stayed any longer, they'd really feel like the mom and dad bringing their baby home. It was hard enough as it was to keep her emotions in check. She forced a confident smile. "If I need you, I'll come and get you."

He nodded, gave another brief look at Ava, then headed off to the rear of the house. The bedroom door closed softly behind him.

Left alone, Violet shrugged out of her suede blazer and rolled up the sleeves on her long-sleeved T-shirt.

She sorted through the baby clothes. Set the wheeled bassinet up with soft cotton linens. Found a place to plug in the bottle warmer and created an impromptu change station at one end of the leather sofa.

She'd just gone in search of the formula and bottles when Ava woke.

The baby's lips pursed into a petulant frown. She looked around and let out a soft whimper.

Violet couldn't blame the little one for being distressed.

After all, Gavin's home was a lot different than the hospital nursery. Her own need to comfort escalating as quickly as Ava's cry, Violet swiftly went to pick the baby up. "I'm right here, darlin'," Violet cooed tenderly, cradling the infant in her arms.

At the sound of her voice Ava relaxed. Her eyes shut and she drifted right back to sleep.

And in that moment Violet knew. She didn't just have a

raging case of baby fever. She had fallen head over heels in love with this little girl and felt very much like her mother. The question was…what *now*?

GAVIN WOKE JUST as it was getting dark. From beyond his bedroom door he could hear the soft, plaintive sound of Ava crying. Blinking himself alert, he threw his legs over the side of the bed and swiftly headed out into the living room.

Violet was in the middle of the front room, swaying slightly, Ava cradled in her arms. She pressed a kiss on the top of the little girl's head. "Hush now, sweetheart. We don't want to wake Gavin."

Heart clenching at the poignant sight, he whispered, "Too late."

She turned, hair swept into a dark silky knot on the back of her head, lips bare. She had spit-up on one shoulder of her T-shirt and a smudge of what looked like baby powder across one cheek. Yet she had never been more beautiful.

She also looked as though she had been through the wringer.

Guilt knotting his gut, he ambled toward her. "How's it been going?" He paused next to them and glanced down at the wide-awake Ava, who was still whimpering.

"Not too bad. As long as I'm holding her and on the move."

Which accounted for Violet's exhausted, harried state.

Gavin wanted to take them both in his arms. Figuring it would be more help, however, to help with Ava, he held out his hands.

Gently, Violet transferred the infant to his waiting arms. "Has she slept?" he asked as Ava snuggled against his chest and shoulder.

"At least a dozen times. The problem is, whenever I try to put her down, she wakes within a minute or two and cries until I pick her up. It doesn't matter whether I settle her in the baby carrier, the bassinet or the buggy. She's unhappy."

Gavin walked back and forth with Ava in his arms. As he did so, her cries subsided and her tiny body relaxed. "She didn't do this in the hospital."

"I know." Violet's glance swept him in a way that made him abruptly aware he was clad only in a pair of boxer-briefs and a T-shirt.

He swore silently. He should have pulled on some pants before coming out here.

Too late now.

Besides, it wasn't as if there wasn't an inch of him she hadn't already seen.

Flushing, Violet cleared her throat and turned her glance away. "Maybe the baby beds there had a different feel to them."

Gavin continued walking back and forth. The baby's eyes fluttered closed, opened, fluttered again. Gently, he rubbed her back, noting that Ava was dressed in a clean onesie, wearing the same knit cotton cap, and was snugly wrapped in a receiving blanket. "She seems warm enough."

Violet came near once again, looking concerned. Standing close enough to Gavin their bodies were touching, Violet caressed the infant's cheek. "And she's dry and fed and burped." She sighed, stepped back slightly, thinking hard. "I just don't think she wants to be put down. At least not in what we have here."

"Okay." Gavin studied the scene with the same cool detachment he assessed a patient who had just been brought into the ER. He handed Ava to Violet, then headed to the bedroom. "I'll take care of it."

Take care of it? Violet let his promise echo in her head. What did that mean? Trying not to notice how sexy and disheveled he looked just out of bed, or to marvel at how tender he was with Ava, she followed him into the bedroom.

"What do you mean?" she asked, frowning as the doorbell rang.

Gavin tugged on his jeans and boots, and threw a shirt on over his T-shirt. He met her anxious glance with a shrug. "I'll see what I can do about getting Ava another bed."

Which would accomplish what? Violet wondered as the bell rang again.

They both walked through the kitchen to the front room. Gavin opened the door. Tara Warren stood on the other side. "Is it a bad time?" LCH's new staff oncologist looked as though she had been crying.

Meanwhile, Ava had gone back to sleep. Violet tenderly cradled the child in her arms. "Not at all. Come on in."

Gavin nodded in greeting. "Hey, Tara." He curved a warm hand over Violet's shoulder. "I'll be back as soon as I can."

She nodded, not at all sure what Gavin was planning to do that was going to help. But she had to let him try. She shut the door behind Tara. "So what's up?" she asked her fellow oncologist.

"I don't know if you've heard, but over half your former patients are refusing to see me."

"That doesn't sound…"

"Good?" Tara teared up again. "It isn't."

"Did they say why?" Deciding to try to put Ava down yet again, she eased her into the baby buggy and pushed it gently back and forth.

"Apparently you're a hard act to follow. And they've all come to the conclusion that if they hold out, you'll change your mind and decide to stay."

If that wasn't emotional blackmail, Violet didn't know

what was. That also went to prove her sense that she had blurred the boundaries and gotten way too close to all her patients was correct. Violet sighed. "What about Carlson Willoughby?"

"He's decided he's too old to break in a new oncologist. He's at home, waiting to die."

Oh, no. "How is Wanda?"

"Defeated. Resigned. Heartbroken. Upset. She said the only person who had even a smidgen of a chance of talking sense into her husband would be you." Tara began to look a little green around the gills. "She came to the hospital a little while ago and begged me to try to talk some sense into you."

Violet rolled the buggy into the kitchen and took out a sleeve of saltines. She handed them to Tara. "I'm sorry."

Tara opened the package and munched on one. "I'm a good doctor, Violet."

"Obviously." Still pushing the buggy back and forth, she took out some ginger ale. "Or you wouldn't have been hired."

Tara took a seat at the table. "I've never had patients react to me this way."

Violet sat, too. Still rocking Ava gently, she soothed, "It's not your fault. It's a pitfall that comes with working in a rural county. Everyone knows everyone else. The bonds that are forged are deep and long-lasting."

"That's why my husband and I wanted to move here. We wanted to raise our family in a small-town environment. But if I can't make inroads with the people here..." Tara shook her head, looking on the brink of tears again.

"Do you want me to talk to the Willoughbys and the other patients again?"

"Would you?"

"I'll have to work it in around caring for Ava, but yes, I'd be happy to."

"Thanks." Tara stood.

Violet put her arm around her. "We'll find a way to work this out." And in the process get the boundaries that should have been set up all along reinstated.

To VIOLET'S SURPRISE, a victorious Gavin passed Tara on the porch.

The oncologist did a double take. "Is that a...?"

Gavin hefted the small bed as if it was nothing. "Hospital nursery bassinet?" He winked. "Yes, it is."

Waving goodbye to Tara, Violet followed Gavin inside, shutting the door behind them. "How did you manage that?" She kept her voice low, so as not to wake the still-sleeping Ava.

He set the wheeled infant bed down against the wall, well away from any draft, straightened and dusted off his hands. "I threw myself on the mercy of the nurses."

Violet planted her hands on her hips and shook her head at the tall, imposing man standing in front of her. "I'm surprised they let you walk out with that."

He chuckled. "They probably wouldn't have had the chief of pediatrics not been there to okay it on a temporary emergency basis."

Oh, dear heaven. Violet cringed. "My *mother* knows about this?"

He draped his arm around her shoulders and pulled her in, his body heat every bit as soothing as his sturdy presence. No wonder Ava had calmed as soon as Gavin had held her in his arms.

"Your mom said she'd come over to help out but they were getting ready to deliver a high-risk infant by C-section. She said to call one of your sisters instead, if this—" he inclined his head at the infant bed "—doesn't work. And, for the record, she seemed to think it wouldn't."

"Why not?"

He strode to the window and looked out toward the street. "Apparently most newborns and new parents have a little trouble adjusting their first twenty-four hours at home." He turned and slid her a look. "Not that we're new parents, exactly."

It felt like it, though. And that was probably precisely why her mother had wanted them to have a chaperone. Violet flashed a grim smile and worked to curtail her mounting aggravation. "I don't need their help."

Gavin consulted his watch. "That's what I said. Still, I wish I didn't have to go in tonight."

"I'll be fine." Violet looked at the buggy, where Ava was stirring again. With a sigh, she began easing it slowly back and forth.

Outside, a car door sounded. "What's that?" she whispered.

"Hopefully, dinner," Gavin murmured in the same low tone. Soundlessly, he eased open the front door. "I called for takeout on the way back here."

Sure enough, the local Italian Villa restaurant delivery car was parked at the curb. Gavin hustled out to the sidewalk and returned with three white paper bags. As he neared, Violet caught the whiff of something delicious.

He read her mind. "Lasagna Bolognese, house salad with Italian, focaccia bread and tiramisu." He carried the bags to the table and set them down. "I hope you're hungry."

"Starved. Thank you."

He bussed her temple and gave her shoulder a squeeze. "Hey. Who am I if I don't take care of my women?"

If only they were both his family.

Pushing her wistfulness aside, she patted his bicep and teased in the same amiable tone, "Gallant to the core."

Basking in the compliment, he brought out the plates and silverware. Violet parked the buggy within reach of the table and took two bottles of water from the fridge.

Together, they sat. No sooner had they ladled food onto their plates than Ava opened her eyes, looked around and began to cry.

A curl of exhaustion swept through Violet. Was this why new mothers looked so worn-out?

Still fresh from his post-work nap, Gavin said, "You eat first."

"You have to go to work."

"Not for three hours. Plenty of time."

Violet couldn't deny she needed fuel. Nor did she want to waste time arguing, so—albeit a little guiltily—she dug in while he got up to feed and change Ava.

By the time she had finished gulping her meal, Ava was asleep. Gavin handed her to Violet. This time she bypassed the baby buggy and settled Ava in the borrowed bassinet, then sat opposite Gavin.

And this time, to their amazement, Ava stayed asleep.

"What do you know," Violet mused, "the right crib was all she needed." Well, that and a little cuddling from Gavin, the daddy figure in her life.

Chapter Ten

"Are you sure you want me to go to work tonight?" Gavin asked when the dishes were done.

Although Ava had been asleep for the past hour, she was starting to stir again; it was nearly time for her next feeding. The baby had been home only ten hours and Violet already looked exhausted.

Gavin paused just outside the laundry closet on the other side of the kitchen, clean towel in hand. "I could call around to see if I can get someone to switch shifts with me."

For a second Violet hesitated, as if almost tempted to take him up on the offer. But she waved off his concern as she walked to the fridge for a bottle of prepared formula. "Don't be silly. You go ahead and get your shower or whatever it was you were planning to do. We'll be fine."

Realizing he was acting more like a brand-new dad than a temporary guardian, and that Violet was suddenly looking as if she were feeling a little crowded in the small space he called home, Gavin nodded.

The plan hadn't been to do this together, but rather in shifts. Hence, he took his time shaving and showering. As he dressed, all seemed calm—at least from what he could hear on his side of the bedroom door. Finally, he eased open the door and emerged.

Violet had baby Ava propped against her shoulder, as if attempting to burp her, and was walking the intermittently fussing infant back and forth. She was, in that instant, the picture of the brand-new mom. Her face was flushed with a combination of fatigue and joy, her hair swept up in a messy knot on the top of her head. Tendrils escaped to frame her pretty face and the elegant nape of her neck. Boots off, her shirt untucked over her jeans, she was gently rubbing the newborn's back, murmuring softly all the while.

"It's a lot to take in, sweetheart, I know. Big changes happening here, with more to come…"

Wasn't that the truth? Gavin thought, enjoying the view from the vantage point of the galley kitchen.

Who would have known his life could be turned upside down so quickly? Or that he would enjoy everything that was happening this much?

Violet paused in front of the picture window that fronted the house. The blinds were still open and they could see the welcoming lights of other homes on the street.

"Luckily, you're too little and inexperienced to understand everything that is going on," Violet continued thickly. "Because if you did, you would know that you should have had what my sisters and their babies all had today. Family, here to greet you upon your arrival. A big, colorful banner with your name on it. A nursery all set up just for you."

Guilt hit Gavin like a punch to the chest.

Was this what Violet had wanted for Ava? Why she'd gone all out to find a special coming-home outfit for the baby? If so, why hadn't she said something?

Surely she would have known as a single guy, he wouldn't have had a clue.

"But it didn't quite happen that way, did it, little one?" She rested her cheek against the baby's downy-soft head and murmured ruefully, "Instead, you were stuck with two guardians who are severely deficient in the baby skills department."

Gavin winced at the accuracy, at least where he was

concerned. Violet seemed to be picking up the skills she needed fast.

Violet shifted Ava to her other shoulder and walked over to the bookshelves where he kept his family photos. Still oblivious to the fact Gavin was within earshot, she cuddled Ava closer. "But one day, sweetheart, you will go to your forever home." Her voice caught on a little sob that sent an arrow straight to Gavin's heart.

"And I'm sure your new daddy and mommy will give you all of those things." Violet's voice hitched again. "And much, much more."

AVA HAD JUST delivered a resounding burp when Violet heard the bedroom door swing open, followed by heavy male footsteps. She had just enough time to pull herself together before Gavin met up with her and Ava in the living area.

Dressed in the blue hospital scrubs and sneakers he sometimes wore to work, he smelled of soap and mint and the masculine fragrance unique to him.

"You two going to be okay?" His gaze roved her casually.

Forcing herself to be the independent "mom" the situation required, she nodded. "We'll be fine. Our little darlin' is half asleep already now that she's finally gotten the air out of her tummy."

She froze. Had she really said, *"Our little darlin'"* out loud? Given the look on Gavin's face, she had.

"You know what I mean," she corrected hastily.

He was quick to say, "I do." He smiled tenderly. "At least for now."

He stepped back abruptly, looking as if he needed to get a grip on the situation every bit as much as she did. He glanced around for his wallet, phone and keys. "You'll text me if you need anything?"

Not sure she trusted her voice, Violet nodded and

walked him as far as the front door, working to contain herself all the while. "See you tomorrow."

His gaze roved the infant in her arms. Leaning forward, he kissed the top of Ava's head, then Violet's cheek. The affectionate gesture sent an even stronger wave of sentimentality roaring through her.

He looked at her for a long moment. "I'll be back as soon as I can," he vowed softly.

"Really," Violet stressed again, ignoring the tears gathering behind her eyes, "we'll be fine."

Except, as it happened, as the very long night wore on, she and Ava weren't exactly fine.

The little darlin' ate, burped and took care of business, waiting with increasing patience through the required diaper changes.

The one thing she would *not* do was sleep for more than five or ten minutes at a time.

Unless she was in Violet's arms.

And though, as a physician, Violet was used to going without sleep, by dawn she was so weary she could barely hold her head up.

The wimpy part of her wanted to call for reinforcements. Or at least to phone her mother or sisters for advice.

But since her parents already thought she'd made the wrong decision in electing to stay at Gavin's, instead of their place—where they would have been around to help her—she resisted the urge.

She'd allowed them to rush in and take command once before when Sterling had been sick and she'd been at a loss. She wasn't doing it again.

"Hey, thanks, man," Gavin said to the ER doc who'd come in to cover for him. A real family man, Barry had half a dozen kids and a wife at home.

"No problem." Barry slapped him on the shoulder. "I'm

just surprised you were able to make it in, given the guardianship thing you have going on."

He probably *shouldn't* have come in, Gavin thought guiltily.

His fellow physician shrugged on his white coat. "Is Violet doing okay?"

Hard to tell, he thought, given the fact that she hadn't answered a single one of his texts all night. "I haven't heard differently," he said, embarrassed to admit just how worried he was, never mind how little Violet had leaned on him thus far. He'd expected this experience to bring them closer, but instead they seemed suddenly further apart than they had ever been.

A fact that made him feel like even more of a failure in the relationship zone. As if, maybe, he really *didn't* have a romantic bone in his body?

Barry looped a stethoscope around his neck. "Then they're probably both sleeping. At least for a few hours at a time."

Gavin hoped that was the case. His gut told him otherwise. Fortunately, thanks to Bridgette and Meg Carrigan, and a whole host of others, he was armed with knowledge on what to do next.

As he suspected, Violet was wide-awake when he walked in, an hour later, carrying a rocking chair that had seen its fair share of fussy babies.

Unable to completely mask her happiness to see him, she blinked. "Where did you get that?"

He removed his jacket and went to wash his hands before taking the baby. "From Erin," he said, easing Ava from her arms.

Violet stood, looking a little woozy. "You left work and drove all the way out to the ranch to get it?"

"I left work to make sure the two of you are okay. Not to worry…I'm going back in at six this evening to finish out the rest of my sub's shift. And Mac, Erin's husband, met me halfway with the chair. So it wasn't that much of a drive for either of us. She been fussing like this long?"

She returned his gaze, her expression carefully shuttered. "On and off, all night. I think she's just overtired."

Was the puffy redness around Violet's eyes from tears? Wishing he'd been there to hold her, he murmured, "So are you, from the looks of it."

Swaying on her feet, Violet walked to the kitchen and poured herself a glass of water from the tap. "Ha-ha."

He followed her, an increasingly sleepy Ava still cradled in his arms. "I'm serious. When was the last time she had a bottle?"

Her brow furrowed warily. "Thirty minutes ago."

"A diaper change?"

Violet sighed. "Five minutes after that."

Gavin looked down at the little darlin' in his arms. Ava was struggling to hold her eyes open. "Has she burped?"

Another long beleaguered sigh. "Twice."

He nodded with the force of his newfound knowledge. "Then it's time."

She looked at him in consternation. "For...?"

"Swaddling."

"Swaddling," Violet repeated, not sure whether to be relieved Gavin had come to rescue them or insulted. It would have been one thing had she not failed so miserably all night long to ace this whole temporary mommy thing or sent out an SOS. She hadn't.

For reasons she didn't completely understand, she wanted to be as competent in this arena as every other, especially in Gavin's eyes.

She wanted him to think what a great mother she was—and just how nuts was that? It wasn't as if they were anything to each other but friends, and bed buddies, and even those two things might be short-term.

So why did it matter if he thought she was marriage material or not?

They weren't headed down that road. And given how different they were, would never be.

Still, it was worth seeing where all this action was headed.

Her emotions in turmoil, Violet watched as Gavin handed Ava back to her and then strode away just long enough to spread a receiving blanket out on the sofa and fold back one corner. He took Ava, carried her over to the blanket and gently placed her so her shoulders were along the fold. Soothing her gently all the while, he brought one triangle of the blanket over across her body, lifting Ava's arm so it was free. He then tucked that end of the blanket beneath her. The other end of the triangle was brought back across her body and tucked in behind her. He pulled the bottom of the blanket up across her tiny feet and tucked it in, too.

"Where did you learn to do that?" Violet asked, feeling rather awestruck. Gavin took a seat in the rocking chair, cuddling the swaddled Ava in his arms. "Last night at the hospital. I was telling some of the nurses about our problem, between patients…"

Violet winced.

He continued rocking, slowly and gently. "'Course, they'd already heard about it—"

Ava's eyes were already drifting shut.

"—because of the fact I had borrowed a bed from the hospital. And someone asked had I taken the newborn care class that the hospital offers. And of course I hadn't."

Violet perched on the edge of the sofa, kitty-corner from him, unable to help but admire his newfound skill as a daddy. Even if it was a woefully temporary one. "Me, either."

"So one of the pediatric nurses on duty showed me some tricks. Swaddling being the most important."

Lo and behold… Violet gasped. "She's asleep." Soundly, it seemed.

"Here goes." Rising smoothly, Gavin gingerly transferred Ava to her bed. He freed his hand from beneath her while keeping the one on her chest there, barely touching, gently comforting.

A minute passed. Then another. Ava didn't move. Violet barely breathed. Finally, Gavin eased his hand away and stepped back. Waited. Still nothing. Ava slept on. And on. And on. The ache in Violet's throat intensified.

"Well, I'll be darned. It really does work," Gavin whispered when another five minutes had passed. He turned to her.

"Good work, 'Dad,'" Violet said. And, to her horror, promptly burst into tears.

GAVIN HAD FIGURED Violet would appreciate his efforts. To find he had added to her distress, crushed him. "Hey, what's wrong?" He gathered her in his arms.

Violet laid her head against his chest. "It's just been a long twenty hours."

"It's more than that," he insisted quietly. She just didn't want to tell him.

And that was okay, too.

For now.

As long as she let him comfort her.

Stroking his hands through her hair, he brushed away her tears, then tilted her face up to his. And in that instant, her mood changed. Her irises darkened. Her whole body leaned into his.

He moved in to claim the kiss. Whispered, "Are you sure about this?"

She gazed at him, as if realizing the same thing he had—that whatever this was starting up between them was beginning to be very, very good. "Oh, yes."

Her hands moved from his chest to his shoulders and clasped behind his neck. With a soft, breathy sigh, she rose on tiptoe and fused her lips to his.

Basking in the gentle surrender of her body, he kissed her deeply, savoring the warmth of her body, the evocative taste of her tongue. As the softness of her breasts pressed against his chest, he inhaled the sweet scent of her skin and the lingering fragrance of her perfume.

Blood thundered through his veins.

Her hips pressed against his.

And still it wasn't enough.

Kissing wildly, they danced their way through the kitchen, as far as the laundry closet. Impatient, he pressed her up against the dryer.

She smiled, knowing exactly what he had in mind.

One by one, the buttons on her shirt came undone. He spread it open, revealing a pale blue bra. Her nipples were jutting through the lace. Lust poured through him, more potent than ever. "You're beautiful."

He eased the clothing from her, then worked on the zipper of her jeans. She moaned a low, desperate, hungry sound as he eased those off, too. Hooking his thumbs in the elastic of her panties, he tugged them down her thighs, just low enough to allow him to slide his palm between them.

She moaned and slipped her hands beneath his shirt, moving them up his spine, all the while kissing him feverishly.

He stroked, explored, caressed.

Their hearts kicked into a heavy beat and everything within them tightened with need.

Violet knew she was losing not just her head—but the

protective shield around her heart—even as he lifted her onto the dryer. She didn't care. Her emotions were in tatters. This was the one thing, the *only* thing that would make her feel better.

And if it helped him, too, she thought wistfully as he shed his clothes and stepped between her thighs... All the better.

He brought her closer, anchoring her legs around his waist. And still they kissed and kissed. He rubbed up against her, so big and strong and blatantly male. Intimately stroked and touched, every move, every caress so incredibly tender and sweet. A sigh rippled through her and then a moan. Dampness flowed. He was deliciously hard, everywhere, and she was ready. So ready...

She cradled his hips within hers. "Gavin..."

Lower still, there was burgeoning pressure and heat.

He throbbed between the tender, knowing ministrations of her hands. "Now?"

She caught her breath at the darkly possessive intent in his tone. "Now."

He held her eyes for a long moment, then slid home. She cried out, softly this time, urgently. He lowered his head and kissed her. For the moment ignoring the way she arched against him, needing that movement, needing...him.

Needing this.

Until he finally began to move.

Slowly, sensually. Hands holding her still, he forced her to submit to the easy, hopelessly erotic, endless strokes. Deep. Then shallow. Then deep and even once again.

And still he kissed her, capturing her lips and tongue, showing her all the ways to taste and savor, love and experience.

Their breathing grew hot and heavy, their bodies slick with sweat.

Excitement escalated. Until at last there was nothing

but passion, desperation, need, all the emotion of the past few weeks overtaking them.

When it was over, they sagged against each other. Spent. Breathless.

And Violet knew it wasn't just her body she had surrendered to Gavin, but her heart.

As VIOLET SNUGGLED against him, Gavin realized two things. One, making love with her was the most amazing thing he had ever experienced. And two, the feelings between them were a lot stronger than compatibility, shared responsibility and lust.

Feeling her body sag with fatigue, Gavin lifted Violet into his arms and carried her to his bed. Instead of settling, she started to rise. "The baby…"

"I'll check on her." Gavin ambled out to the living room.

When he returned, their abandoned clothes in hand, Violet was sitting on the edge of the bed. She looked deliciously tousled. And, to his disappointment, way too fatigued to make love again. "Why don't you sleep?"

"I should get dressed first."

Or not, he thought, liking the idea of her naked, in his bed. But realizing she might be warmer clothed, he asked, "Where's your suitcase?"

Her kiss-swollen lips twisted wryly. "At the stablehouse. I was so excited about going to the hospital to pick up Ava, I forgot to put it in my car."

He went into his closet and took out one of his buttondown shirts. "Will this do?"

She looked at the soft cotton longingly. "You sure?"

Was she kidding? "One of my fantasies come true," he teased.

She offered a weak smile and let him help her on with it. "This is becoming a habit."

One he highly enjoyed. Tenderness flowing through

him, he guided her lovingly down to the pillows. "You need to rest," he repeated his earlier admonition. "I'll handle Ava. And if not, she'll let you hear about it."

"True." Violet chuckled and shut her eyes.

Seconds later, she was fast asleep.

Gavin stood, watching her, something warm and soft unfurling in his heart. And in that instant he knew something else. That what had started out to be a temporary fling had turned into much, much more.

The question was did Violet realize it, too?

Chapter Eleven

Violet awakened with a start five hours later. She jumped up, for a second not sure where she was. And then she remembered. Gavin's house. Gavin's bed.

And Ava…where was she? Violet wondered anxiously. *How was she?*

She padded barefoot to the bedroom door.

Easing it open, she saw Gavin standing in the kitchen. While she'd been sleeping, he'd changed into snug-fitting jeans and a white, short-sleeved T-shirt that did equally disturbing things to his washboard abs. He had a burp cloth thrown over one broad shoulder, a wide-eyed Ava, clad in a fresh pink onesie, cuddled in his arms. Together, they were the picture of doting father and his newborn daughter.

As her gaze drifted over them, memorizing the moment for all time, Violet found herself awash in sentiment.

How was she ever going to give all this up and just walk away when, despite the hardships of settling in, it felt like one long, unbelievably happy dream?

The kind she thought had eluded her.

"Well, look who's awake," Gavin drawled, his sensual glance drifting over her.

Awake and lusting for a kiss. A hug. More scintillating sex. But that was all fantasy, too, Violet reminded herself, rubbing her eyes.

They had joined together to be temporary guardians. That was all.

Eventually they were going to have to let Ava go and move on, no matter how difficult that proved. It might be better if she were prepared for that.

"Or *are* you awake?" Gavin teased, hitting the button on the bottle warmer, then strolling closer. He bent to kiss her brow and shook his head in bemusement. "You still look a little dreamy…"

Not to mention, as hopelessly idealistic as ever, Violet thought, still breathless from the brief caress. *Wishing so hard for everything to be perfect that for a moment I imagined it actually was.*

Gavin's gaze drifted to the upper curve of her breasts.

Abruptly, she realized she probably should have put on something more than her panties and his pale blue shirt. Probably brushed her hair, too.

With his arms still full of baby, he leaned closer and nuzzled the top of her head. "Sure you don't want to go in and get another three or four hours of shut-eye?" His glance darkened protectively. "I don't have to go back until six tonight."

"That's right. You're working the other half of the shift you cut short last night."

He nodded. "I'll be back at midnight, though. And then I don't have to work again for forty-eight hours."

"Was that the original schedule?"

"I switched some things around so I could be here more to help out with Ava." He studied her closely. "Is that okay?"

Was he kidding? Yet another fantasy come true. Except she had a few work items to handle. Starting with that long list of calls to the patients who were giving Tara Warren a hard time.

Aware she was tingling everywhere, and they hadn't

even touched, Violet fought a blush. "I can handle the close quarters if you can."

She wasn't sure she could make love with him again— which they surely would if they were in close quarters— and not fall in love with him. But that was a dilemma for another time, she decided. Right now she was going to enjoy the moment. The baby. The man.

"It's only for a month or so," he said with a shrug.

"Right." Which was a soul-crushing limit she hadn't wanted to think about.

Aware she was on the edge of another emotional crying jag, Violet inhaled deeply and looked past him to the foyer. "Is that my suitcase?"

"I asked Poppy to bring it for you. She dropped it off a while ago. And as long as you're up, your cell phone has been going off since noon."

Violet went to check and found a dozen text messages.

"They fixed the plumbing problem at McCabe House."

He came closer. "Great."

Trying not to notice how big and hard and strong he was, all over, she said, "I've got about ten offers to baby-sit Ava for us."

He grinned, giving her a sexy once-over. "Also good if we want to go out to dinner or something."

Was he asking her for a date? Her heart skipped a beat at the possibility. Although what exactly that meant...

"And an email from the San Antonio Medical Center."

He waited, his expression impassive.

To her surprise, Violet felt similarly discombobulated. She read it. "They've offered me a staff physician position in their oncology department."

It wasn't really a surprise. She'd known by what was said at her interview the month before that she was a leading candidate for the position.

What was a shock was that the joy she had expected

to feel, if this position did in fact materialize for her, was nowhere to be found.

Gavin paused. "What's the proposed start date?"

A lot sooner than she had planned, unfortunately. Violet exhaled slowly and lifted her face to his. "One month from today."

His expression grew even more inscrutable. "Are you going to take it?"

She had all the reasons in the world to say yes. So why was she hesitating? "I, uh, want to make sure Ava is settled first."

"And then?" he asked, still the epitome of masculine calm.

She didn't know. "I'm still waiting to hear back on a couple more positions that I interviewed for. So I'll wait and see."

"THAT MEANS," GAVIN explained to Ava, when Violet went off to get a shower, "we still have a chance to convince her to stay right here in Laramie."

Her eyes on him, Ava drank from her bottle.

"The hospital needs her," Gavin continued. *I need her.*

Where had that thought come from?

He shifted the baby in his arms so she could more easily access the formula. "You need her, too," he said softly. "At least until we find your permanent home."

And they all moved on.

Which, given how quickly and deeply emotionally involved he and Violet both were becoming in this child's life, couldn't happen a moment too soon.

Because heaven knew it would be almost impossible to give the child up if either of them got any more attached to her than they currently were.

Fortunately, Mitzy Martin stopped by just after Violet emerged from the bedroom, fresh from the shower.

Her hair fell down her back in a damp, silky mass. She smelled of his soap and shampoo, and was dressed in a pair of faded jeans and a knit pine-green shirt that buttoned up the front. Shearling-lined moccasins and socks covered her feet. She hadn't bothered with makeup, which only served to show off the creamy perfection of her fair skin and the whiskey-gold of her eyes. But nothing could mask the slightly fatigued set of her slender shoulders and the shadows beneath her eyes.

"Rough first twenty-four hours at home?" Mitzy asked.

Violet shrugged off the sympathy with her usual grace. "We're getting the hang of it." She looked over at Gavin for support.

He nodded in acknowledgment, at that moment feeling very much like the co-guardianship team they were supposed to be. "Violet's doing a great job."

"So are you," Violet said in return.

Mitzy gave them both an odd look.

Clearly, Gavin thought, this was not what she had expected.

Not wanting to reveal the romantic turn his relationship with Violet had taken—for fear too much scrutiny too soon would ruin their fragile closeness—Gavin handed Ava over to Violet.

Working to get the conversation back on track, he asked Mitzy, "I gather you have some news for us?"

"I do." Mitzy smiled at the newborn, who was now resting her head on Violet's shoulder, trying to work up a burp as Violet gently rubbed her back.

"I have a file full of videos from all the interested adoptive parents and families." Mitzy pulled a CD with Ava's name on it out of her briefcase. She handed it to Gavin.

"As you know, the waiting list for infants is extremely long, so home studies have already been done on all of the perspective candidates on the disc. So anyone you see in the group would be readily approved by the court. It's really a matter of which family you think would be the best fit for her."

"We'll look at them right away," Gavin promised. Even though it felt as if he was doing Ava a disservice in sending her to live with someone else.

"Great." Mitzy beamed her relief. "I thought we would have you pick the top three prospects and then introduce Ava to the families to see who is the most compatible."

"Sounds easy enough," Violet said lightly.

Except it wouldn't be for her, Gavin thought, if he was reading her emotions accurately. And not for him, either.

"Will we be able to read through the background information on the applicants before we decide?" Violet asked, her expression matter-of-fact.

"Absolutely," Mitzy reassured her. "We want you to feel completely comfortable with whichever family you choose to be Ava's parents."

"You look stressed out," Gavin observed after Mitzy left.

Whereas he, she thought, looked relaxed as could be. Violet ignored the river of emotion pouring through her. She went into the kitchen to do the dishes and found there were none to do. Gavin had already taken care of that, too.

So she stood, with her hands braced on the edge of the sink, looking out the window at the street.

Leaves were beginning to change.

Going from green to gold, brown and red.

Violet swallowed around the ache in her throat. "It's a big responsibility." And one she still didn't really want. How was she supposed to pick a family for the child she wanted to bring up herself? And wasn't thinking that way selfish? When she and Gavin had agreed from the outset they would do what was best for Ava and give her over to a loving, stable family to raise?

His hands on her shoulders, Gavin turned her to face him. A day's growth of beard gave him a rugged, manly appearance. He brushed his thumb across the curve of her cheek. "Is that all?"

Of course he saw right through her. He always did. Trying not to let his tenderness undo her composure, Violet inhaled a shaky breath. "I promised Tara I would go over to see Carlson and Wanda today."

"You want me to go with you or to watch Ava?"

Resisting the urge to throw herself in his arms, Violet extricated herself from his grip and leaned against the counter. Their gazes locked and she felt another moment of tingling awareness.

She cleared her throat. "Actually, I thought I'd take Ava with me. The Willoughbys live just a few streets over. It's a nice afternoon." The fresh air might help her clear her head of all these ridiculously romantic notions. "I could put Ava in the buggy and stroll her over while you rest a while before your next shift."

To her relief, Gavin didn't argue. "Okay. I'll leave my cell phone on if you need me to come get her."

Violet nodded her thanks. She paused, aware her emotions were still a little raw. "About those videos Mitzy left... Tomorrow or the day after is soon enough to watch them, don't you think?"

He smiled gently. "We can go over them together when we have a little more time."

Relieved to be able to put that task aside, at least for the moment, Violet settled Ava in the buggy and readied to walk over to the Willoughbys' home.

"I THOUGHT I'D stop by to say hello," Violet said when Wanda opened the door and stepped out onto the porch of the bungalow.

Today's athletic suit was dark brown. The reading

glasses she wore could not hide the redness around her eyes. It looked as if she had been crying. Given the situation, it was easy to understand why.

"Oh, you brought the baby!" The older woman walked down the steps to peer into the buggy, where Ava slept soundly. "I heard you and Dr. Monroe were taking care of a little one together."

"Temporarily," Violet said.

Wanda laid a hand over her heart. "Well, she's just darling!"

That, Ava was, with her dark lashes resting against her soft, pink cheeks, and her rosebud lips pursed in a sweet little pout.

"It's too bad the two of you can't keep her."

Yes, it was.

"But given the fact you're not married, well…"

"It makes sense to find her a family with two loving parents," Violet said.

Wanda nodded her understanding.

A brief silence fell.

Violet got straight to the point. "I talked with Dr. Warren."

Carlson walked out to join them. "Then you know I'll only go through with treatment if you are here to administer it, Dr. McCabe."

Violet wasn't surprised to see nothing had changed. The old man was as stubborn as he was smart. "Dr. Warren is an excellent doctor."

Wanda dug in all the more. "*You're* the one we trust."

"Which is a problem in and of itself," Violet said with sincere regret. "I've done you a grave disservice if I've left you with the impression that I'm the only member of the medical team you can trust. All the doctors, the nurses, the radiologists and aides contribute to the excellent care you receive."

"You're saying we should trust Dr. Warren."

"She would never have been hired if she weren't top-notch."

Wanda shook her head. "But she's not family to us. You're family, Dr. McCabe. And we only want family looking after Carlson."

Violet sucked in a breath. "Then give her a chance. Let her become family to you, too."

"You should be flattered they think so highly of you," Gavin said after he had woken from his nap and she'd told him about her meeting with the Willoughbys.

Violet sorted baby clothes, then put the pastels in the washer. "If I'd really been doing my job, they'd trust more than just me."

He sent her an intuitive glance. "What's really going on here?"

Violet measured baby laundry detergent into a cup. "It's too much pressure."

Gavin disappeared into the bathroom and returned with an electric razor. "You've been handling it so far."

Trying not to think what they had done in this very laundry area just a few hours before, Violet selected a warm-water cycle. "Because up until now, I kept some boundaries and emotional distance from them."

He ran the razor over his jaw. "Your ability to care about your patients is what makes you such a good physician."

It would be so easy to lean on him this way.

Violet released a shuddering breath. With difficulty, she met his probing blue gaze. "It can also cause me to lose my perspective and blind me to what's really going on, if I'm not careful."

He moved the razor to the other side of his face. "When has that happened?"

Violet piled the baby whites, still waiting to be washed,

back into the hamper. "With Sterling. He was sick off and on for almost a year before he ever came out and told anyone." Satisfied the soap was integrating nicely in the water, she closed the lid and raised a hand before Gavin could say anything that would let her off the hook. "I was living with him. I should have seen the signs and understood what it all meant, forced him to go to a doctor a lot sooner."

Gavin's brow furrowed. "You were both just medical students at the time, weren't you?"

Violet followed him to the closet where he pulled out a clean pair of scrubs. "I still should have known something was wrong, whether he admitted it to himself or not." Guilt knotted her gut. "Wanda knew something was going on with Carlson, long before he was first diagnosed. She made him go to the doctor to get checked out. Because of that, his cancer was detected early." A lump rose in her throat. "I didn't do that for Sterling."

A silence fell. Once again, he saw far more of what she was thinking and feeling than she would have wished. "Is that the real reason you want to leave Laramie?" he asked softly, stripping off his jeans. "You're afraid you'll miss something with the patients you're close to?"

She averted her gaze from the soft covering of dark hair on his legs. "Part of it is still Sterling." She folded her arms tightly in front of her. "This is where I did the bulk of my grieving. So being here sometimes makes me sad."

"But?"

She watched as he tugged on a scrub shirt and pulled it down over his broad shoulders and sinewy chest. "I am scared I'm too personally involved and that I will miss something." Her chin quavered as she looked into his eyes and let herself spill all. "I couldn't bear it if that happened."

He took her into his arms. Holding her close, he stroked her cheek. "Why do you think that might happen?"

Her breath hitched in her throat. She pulled away and

began to pace. "Because when you care about someone, you don't want to admit there could be something really wrong. Instead, you look for ways to reassure yourself and your loved one that there isn't anything amiss, that it's just stress or fatigue causing them not to feel well."

He listened in a way that made it easier for her to go on.

"Coming back to Laramie to do my residency, after Sterling died, was helpful to me. I was closer to family and surrounded by people I cared about and had known all my life. But—" she took another breath and forced herself to continue "—when I became the oncologist to some of those same people, those feelings of affection and concern for their well-being deepened."

"So you're not leaving because you care too little. You're leaving Laramie because you care too much," he surmised softly.

Violet nodded.

He wrapped an arm around her shoulders and kissed the top of her head. "Does anyone else know this?" he asked, giving her a comforting squeeze.

Violet bit her lip. "Not really. I mean, I talked to my parents about it a while back, when I first started noticing I could have a problem. They told me it was something all doctors experience to some degree, and that as time goes on, I'll learn how to detach enough to do my job."

He led her over to sit on the edge of his bed. "And have you?"

Violet looked up at him. "Not as much as I feel I need to."

As he sat beside her, their legs came in contact from thigh to knee. He did not move away. "The same thing could happen if you go elsewhere."

Violet didn't move away, either. "It'll be different if I'm treating strangers instead of people and families I've known my entire life."

"Don't kid yourself about that," he scoffed. "I've had it happen to me, too."

Violet shifted slightly toward him. "As an ER doc?" she asked in surprise.

"I'm treating people I've known forever, too. It's true, a lot of them only come in once—because they're having a heart attack or stroke or have been in a car accident. But as I told you before, I also have patients I see a lot more frequently." His voice turned quiet, more somber. "There's a kid with cystic fibrosis who may not live a whole lot longer who breaks my heart every time. An older gentleman whose diabetes is out of control. ALS and muscular dystrophy patients who can get very ill, very fast."

For the first time Violet thought not just about their differences but all they had in common, too. As people. As doctors. "So what do you do?" she asked, her respect for him growing all the more.

He shrugged. "I focus on the problem at hand and don't let myself think about anything else."

Silence fell as they sat there a moment, side by side, before Violet flicked another glance his way. "You still don't think I should leave Laramie."

He shook his head, his expression grave. "You're needed here."

She grinned at the ferocity of his determination. "By the community."

"And by me," he told her, shifting her onto his lap and kissing her softly.

As she kissed him back, a mixture of desire and longing for even more swept through her. If only they could fall in love.

If only the situation were ideal…

He stroked a hand through her hair and pulled back to look into her eyes. He kissed the back of her hand, the inside of her wrist. "And if I didn't have to go to work in about five minutes, I'd show you just how much you are wanted."

Her heart skittered in her chest. *Wanted* was good. So was *needed*. But she wanted to be loved, too. Was that too much to ask?

"Are you okay?" he asked, eyeing her carefully.

Was she? With Ava to care for, Violet knew she had only one option. "Of course I am," she said.

She had to be, so she would be.

Chapter Twelve

"Thanks for bringing dinner," Violet said two hours later when her mom and dad stopped by to check on her and Ava.

Her father set a bag from the local barbecue restaurant on the table in the living area. "We were happy to do it."

Her mother went straight to the wicker bassinet, where Ava was now sleeping. She gazed tenderly down at the infant. "No more hospital crib?"

Gavin had taken the borrowed infant bed back to the hospital. "It wasn't the bed she was sleeping in that was the problem," Violet admitted, chagrined. "She just needed to be swaddled to feel secure."

Moving away, her mother said gently, "You could have called me when you were having difficulty."

And risk being a failure in their eyes? Knowing she had done enough to earn their disapproval in the past, Violet merely nodded. "Next time."

The three of them sat down to dinner. Her dad sent her a curious look. "How is the search for an adoptive family going?"

Almost too smoothly, Violet thought, aware she was less eager to finish her task with every minute that had passed. "Earlier today Mitzy dropped off a list of potential candidates to review."

While her parents passed around savory platters of

tender smoked turkey breast, coleslaw, potato salad and green beans, Violet went on to explain the process. She reached into her purse to retrieve her computer tablet. "But that's not really why I asked you over tonight," she said. "I wanted to talk to you about the job offer I received from San Antonio."

After reviewing the email, Lacey and Jackson agreed it was an excellent offer. "Are you going to take it?" her mother asked.

Two weeks ago, she would have.

But everything was different now.

Violet swallowed. "I was thinking that I might stay on in Laramie and continue to work for the hospital for another six months or maybe even a year."

To her disappointment, the joy she had expected to see on her folks' faces was not there.

Her father frowned, in chief-of-staff mode now. "It depends on why you're making the decision."

"Part of it is the patients," Violet explained, cutting into a slice of turkey. "They all seem to think I'm letting them down by not staying on to see them transition to Dr. Warren's care."

"And the rest?" her mother asked gently.

"Is my commitment to help out at McCabe House—"

"The rest of the family can pitch in to handle that," her father interjected.

"I know, but there is Ava's situation, too." Violet took a sip of iced tea, then stared down at her plate. "It's turning out to be more complicated than I expected."

Her parents exchanged looks. "Have you changed your mind about relinquishing your guardianship and placing her with someone else?" her mother asked finally. "Because as we told you earlier, we would support that."

"I can't do it on my own, Mom."

"So you've changed your mind and Gavin hasn't changed his?" Lacey mused, putting down her fork.

Since there was no way to honestly and adequately answer that, given the fact she and Gavin hadn't come out and talked about it, she said instead, "We both want what's best for little Ava."

Her mother resumed eating. "What about what's best for you?"

The bite of creamy potato salad Violet had just taken lodged like a stone in her tummy. Lifting her chin, she tried for calm. "What do you mean?"

Grave looks passed between her parents. With a worried sigh, her mother admitted, "We don't want to see you in the same situation you were in before. Tying yourself to someone who does not have the same level of commitment to you—or to Ava—that you have to them."

GAVIN WASN'T SURPRISED to see Violet's dad that evening. The chief of staff had been called in to perform emergency surgery on a car accident victim with a broken leg. He didn't expect to have an unsettling conversation with him and he was still thinking about what Jackson had said as he drove home.

Violet had left the porch light on. The interior lights were still blazing, too. Gavin let himself in.

A little after midnight, Ava was in her bassinet, sleeping. Violet was busy making up a bed on the sofa. She turned to him with a bright smile that didn't quite reach her eyes.

"I don't know if you had a chance to eat dinner yet, but my parents brought over barbecue. There's plenty left, in the fridge."

He nodded his thanks. "How did your talk with them go?" he asked casually. Able to see she was about to evade, he added, "Better than mine with your dad, I hope?"

Her cheerful facade faded. An unsettling silence fell between them. "He talked to you?"

"A few minutes ago, at the hospital."

She grabbed a pillow and slid on a new case. "About?"

"Us taking the long view and not acting on our temporary emotions."

She dropped the pillow onto the sofa, mouth set. "Let me guess. He also referenced my misguided, overly idealized sense of responsibility toward others."

He helped her spread the blanket over the sheet. "How did you know?"

She placed her hand over her heart, the other tucked against her ribs. "It's an old argument."

He took a stab in the dark. "Having to do with Sterling and the fact you apparently were a whole lot more devoted to him than he was to you?"

Violet turned and paced away. Her shoulders slumping, she ran a weary hand over her eyes. "I wish to heaven they would let that go."

"Then it's true? Your ex didn't love you, at least not the way you loved him."

She moved through the kitchen to the bedroom. "It's complicated."

He watched her rummage through the suitcase. "Meaning you don't want to talk about it."

She disappeared into the bathroom, something flowery clutched in her hand. "I don't want to talk about anything they said to me this evening," she said through the door.

Deciding to use the opportunity to change, he tugged off his scrubs and slid on a pair of low-slung cotton pajama pants and a gray T-shirt. "You mean there was more?"

She walked out, clad in a pair of pink-and-white-flowered flannel pajamas. She looked sexy and sweet as hell. His body reacted as if a match had been lit.

"Heck, yes, there was more!" She gathered her dark hair

and tucked it into a clip on the back of her head. "This is my parents we're talking about!" She marched back into the bathroom again.

Doing his best to tamp down his desire, he lingered in the doorway "Do they still want you to take Ava over to their place?" He watched her spread a creamy white soap over her face while avoiding her lips.

"They think I'm going to get hurt if we continue our current arrangement."

"Because you're getting too close to Ava." They both were, if truth be told. Even he—the guy without a romantic bone in his body—could see it was going to hurt like hell to give Ava up. Although this was what they both had vowed they would do.

Violet bent to rinse her face. His gaze fell to the sexy curve of her hips beneath the flannel—which was now stretched taut, delineating the area he wanted to explore.

"And to you," she admitted reluctantly.

Forcing himself to stop thinking about making love to her, at least for now, Gavin handed her a towel. "You told them we hooked up?"

"No, of course not," she said, clearly irritated by his stunned tone. "But they know me and they know you, and they've deduced that we've suddenly become a whole lot closer to each other by the way we have been interacting." She reached for a bottle of face lotion.

"We're *supposed* to be a team where Ava is concerned."

"I know." Violet spread moisturizer across the elegant planes of her face and neck. She recapped the bottle with a snap and shook her head. "But they think even that has the potential to lead us both astray."

Her parents might have had a point about that, he thought, fighting the rush of guilt deep inside him.

The gentleman in him knew he should have waited until

the situation with the baby was resolved to make love with Violet.

But the man in him knew waiting had been as impossible for her as it was for him. They needed to be together. The shared responsibility of the baby had made it all possible.

"So they don't want to see you with me?" He tamped down the hurt in his voice.

"No, it's not like that." Violet stepped up to him and tenderly stroked his jaw. "They like you, Gavin. They really do."

Hearing the equivocation in her careful words, he felt another punch to his gut. "Then what exactly do they want to see happen?" he asked gruffly.

This time there was a flash of hurt in *her* eyes. Violet swallowed, recalling the rest of her parents' words. "They said they would be *happy* to see me dating you. Or adopting Ava on my own. Even having a baby of my own, as a single mom." She blew out a breath. "What they don't want to see is the three of us getting more and more emotionally entangled just because you and I happened to be named Ava's co-guardians."

"It's more than that upsetting your parents," Gavin insisted. "Tell me."

"Well, if you must know," she said hesitantly, "it's the fact that my bunking with you is so reminiscent of the way that Sterling and I first started sharing space."

Her love for her late fiancé was legendary—at least in Laramie. But there was nothing in the lore that stated there had been any impropriety.

Trying to put the pieces together, Gavin peeked out into the living room, where Ava was still asleep, then went into the kitchen and began fixing himself a plate of food.

"You weren't engaged to Sterling at the time?"

Violet followed him into the kitchen. She reached into the freezer and brought out a small container of Rocky

Road ice cream. "Actually, we weren't even dating. We were just study partners in our first year of med school." She flipped off the lid and took a spoon from the drawer.

"I had my parents' backing and an apartment of my own. Sterling was putting himself through school and sharing a two-bedroom place with four other guys in similar financial straits."

"Sounds okay so far."

Together, they took their food to the dining table.

"We couldn't study there, so more often than not, we ended up at my place. Eventually, he was there so much, it made sense for him to move in and pay a portion of the rent."

Gavin settled next to her. "As your friend."

Their knees bumped under the table. "That's all we were our first year."

Gavin didn't know how in the heck that was possible. Violet was so damn sexy, so loving and pretty and adorably funny, it would be impossible to be that close to her and not fall under her spell. "How did your parents feel about it?"

"They weren't happy we were cohabiting."

Knowing how protective Jackson McCabe was about all six of his daughters, Gavin guessed not.

"Then, somewhere in the middle of the second year, we began to see each other in a different light."

Sort of like what's happened with us.

"One thing led to another. We became a couple."

"And that made your parents happy?" Gavin proposed.

"No. They said we either needed to make a commitment and get married or stop playing house."

"Ouch."

"Yeah. There was so much tension regarding the subject that my folks and I even stopped speaking for a while."

"Understandable. You were an adult."

"And more than capable of making my own decisions,

but Sterling, who'd been abandoned by his dad as a youngster and lost his mom a few years before, regretted having caused the rift between me and my folks." She smiled sadly. "So, just before our third year of medical school started, he asked me out for a special evening. As we got ready to go out, I could tell he wasn't feeling all that great, but he insisted. So we went to this very swanky restaurant in downtown Houston."

"That's where he popped the question?"

She closed her eyes, recalling. "He would have, had he not collapsed shortly after the main course was served."

His heart went out to her. "And that's when you found out he had cancer."

Her grief over that was still apparent. "Widespread metastatic cancer."

Silence fell as he imagined what a traumatic time that had been for them. "So he proposed anyway?"

For a moment he thought she wasn't going to answer. "That's what I told everyone, including my parents, but... no."

He took up his empty plate and followed her into the kitchen. "Then why does everybody think you were engaged?"

She paced, looking more miserable than he'd ever seen her. "Because when I found out that Sterling wanted to call the whole thing off and let me go—for my sake—I took the diamond ring the EMS workers had found in his jacket pocket and given to me for safekeeping while we were en route to the ER. And I proposed to him, right there in the hospital." Her expression grew taut with remembered hurt and disappointment.

Gavin guessed what happened next. It was what he would have done under the circumstances. "He said no?"

A terse nod. "But I said I didn't care what he wanted at that point, or thought he wanted, I wasn't going to let him go. So I slipped that diamond on my finger, pretended everything had gone according to his original plan and told everyone we were going to get married." Her jaw set in the stubborn way he was beginning to know so well. "I had this ridiculous idea that if Sterling knew how very much I loved him, he would magically get better."

"The love and support of friends and family can work miracles." In their profession, they'd both seen it happen time and again.

Violet tilted her face up to Gavin's. "Yes, well…me being me, I couldn't just let it go with a simple commitment of love. I insisted we were going to weather his illness as a *team*."

This was beginning to sound familiar—and not in a good way, Gavin thought.

"So when Sterling had to drop out of med school that semester to undergo treatment, I took a leave from my studies, too."

Ah. No wonder she'd been unable and unwilling to talk to Nicholas for him. She would have had to bring all this up, too. He cupped his hands on her shoulders. "And your parents?"

Violet rubbed the toe of her bare foot across the wood floor. "They did not think I should be doing that. But with all that going on with Sterling, there was no way I could focus on my studies, never mind be involved in patient care."

She had a point. Sensing she needed comfort, Gavin wrapped his arm around her and brought her into the cradle of his body. "What did Sterling think?"

Violet shook her head. "He wanted me to stay in med school. But he was too sick to argue, so, like everything else, he let it go. And let me take care of him—although that, too, was against his better judgment."

Gavin ran a hand up and down her spine. "Why didn't

he want you to care for him?" He watched her face, noting she was looking as if she were beginning to feel a little better now this was all coming out.

Violet sighed. "He found it emasculating, to have to rely on me. And he was disappointed our 'engagement,' such as it was, started out while he was ill."

Gavin could understand that, just as he understood Violet's wish to take care of the man she had loved. "Did he ask you to end your engagement?"

"More than once."

Gavin couldn't stand the raw vulnerability in her low tone. "You refused."

Violet splayed her hands across Gavin's chest. "When I told him I loved him enough to marry him, I meant in sickness and in health. I wasn't going to renege on that."

"So he kept mum?"

Violet took in another halting breath, then stepped away from Gavin. "He didn't really have any choice, unless he wanted to humiliate me publicly, and he was too much of a gentleman for that. Plus, he knew having some concrete symbol of our future together, like the diamond ring and the hope that we *would* one day marry, was a comfort to me. And, maybe, deep down, to him, too. So he let my lie stand."

Gavin could understand that. "And your parents?"

"They knew there was tension between Sterling and me, because I couldn't accept the fact that Sterling wasn't ever going to get better, even when all the tests and scans proved otherwise. But they never knew the truth about our engagement." She sighed heavily. "They still don't."

Just when he thought he couldn't possibly be surprised by her, he was.

"Does anyone?" he asked, curious.

Violet turned troubled eyes to his. "No," she said softly. "I've never told anyone. Until now."

Chapter Thirteen

"Why me?" Gavin asked. "Why now?"

Good question, Violet thought. And one she really didn't want to contemplate, but… "I guess I'm just tired of carrying that secret around." Tired of being alone. Tired of feeling as if she had somehow made a mistake in giving her heart away.

Aware he wanted and needed more from her than that, however, after all she had revealed, she reverted to her usual sly humor as defense.

She looked him up and down, teasing lightly, "And if there was ever anyone who would understand being misunderstood, it would have to be 'the man who doesn't have a romantic bone in his body.' At least, according to your very wrongheaded exes."

Gavin chuckled, seemingly relieved at the newly lightened mood. "What makes you think the women were all wrong about me?" he challenged mildly, looking suddenly as if her dad's talk had gotten to him, leaving him thinking that he wasn't the right man at the right time for her, either.

Determined not to let her ill-fated past cheat her out of another love, she took him by the hand and led him into the bedroom. Instead of heading for the bed, though, she found a place against the wall and backed him up against it. Taking his head in her hands, she rose on tiptoe and fit her lips to his. "This."

With an aggression she'd never dared to let herself unleash before, she pressed her whole body against him and poured every bit of pent-up need and longing that she had into the steamy kiss. And then all was lost in the first thrilling heat of their bodies and mouths.

Violet could tell he hadn't meant to fall for her, any more than she had meant to fall for him. And somehow that made the culmination of their desire all the more scintillating. This wasn't supposed to happen, yet it had. She wasn't supposed to be this reckless or wanton, yet she was.

Gavin groaned, his unbridled hunger coming through loud and clear. Threading his hands through her hair, he lifted his head from hers. "Are you sure this is what you want?" he murmured.

Emotion swept through her like a tsunami, followed by a wealth of need. Lower still, in the feminine heart of her, the tingling started. She slid her hands beneath his shirt and ran her palms across the satiny-smooth muscles. Her breath coming raggedly, she pressed closer still.

"Because if you want or need to wait…until things aren't quite so complicated…I'm on board with that."

It helped. Knowing he would be as patient as she needed. She moved her hands around to his back, up his spine. Kissed his neck, his jaw, each corner of his lips. And felt him shudder in response. "I may want everything to be perfect. But I gave up thinking it would be a long time ago." She undid the first two buttons of her pajama top and lifted it over her head. Standing there in a transparent demi-bra, she drank in the tantalizing scent of soap and man and the masculine fragrance of the cologne he favored. She leaned up and brushed her lips against his once again.

"What I want now is you. Right here." She reached behind her, undid the clasp on her bra and let it slip from her arms. "Like this."

His chest rose and fell with each breath. He shook his head as if wondering at their undeniable passion, too. "You make a very strong case."

Grinning, he switched places with her, so her back was against the wall.

Her knees weakened as he began to kiss her with everything that had been missing in her life.

Yearning. Tenderness. And a need that was so strong and all-encompassing there was no way to describe it.

"Good," she whispered. "Because I want you."

"I want you, too. So much…"

His gray-blue eyes darkening with pleasure, he resumed the hot, heady kiss. She could feel his fierce arousal beneath his pajamas as he took her wrists in hand and pinned them behind her, leaving no doubt as to who was in charge.

Sensations ran riot through her as he teased her nipples into aching crowns, then moved down, sliding his hand beneath the flannel, stroking her through the damp fabric of her panties, until she gasped. "More," she demanded.

"Ah. A woman after my own heart." His free hand slid between them, stroking from pelvis to knee and back again.

She was teetering on the edge of something wonderful… hot and melting inside…

"Gavin," she moaned. Her pajama pants and panties came off. "I'm supposed to be calling the shots."

He chuckled softly and then his mouth was there, with nothing between them, his fingers parting the slick folds, sliding inside her. Making lazy forays, moving in, out and in again.

Driving her crazy as more moisture pooled, making her feel more beautiful and womanly and wanted than she had in her entire life. And then something else was happening. She was trembling, aching, exploding inside with pleasure.

Suddenly he was rising again, shucking off his pants.

Finding a condom and easing between her legs with a blatant masculine resolve that had her surrendering to him all over again.

For a moment Violet didn't think it was going to be possible. He was so big and hot and hard. Too overwhelming. But he did fit, and when inside her, pleasure swept through her, more fierce and enervating than ever before.

Together, trembling, they rose and fell and rose again, then succumbed to the inevitable, swirling bliss. And Violet knew, whatever happened, whatever the future held, no longer mattered. Because this—what they felt...what they brought to each other—would never change.

ALTHOUGH VIOLET HAD planned to sleep on the sofa and to do all the midnight feedings with Ava, the thought of being apart did not sit well with Gavin. So he convinced Violet to wheel the bassinet into the bedroom and place it next to the bed.

That way, when the baby woke, they each could share in the responsibility. One could change the diaper while the other heated the bottle. Both could feed and burp her, and then all three could go back to sleep more quickly.

It was a cozy, familial arrangement.

Even though Gavin knew their time with Ava wasn't going to last, he intended to enjoy every second of it and to make sure Violet did, too.

By morning, unfortunately, the next phase of their guardianship proved more difficult than even he expected.

"This is harder than I thought it was going to be," Violet said when she and Gavin finally sat to review the potential parents for baby Ava. "Do we go with a set of brand-new parents who, like us, has little or no experience in the practical aspects of caring for an infant? Or choose a family that has already brought up an infant? In which case, Ava would have a brother or sister or both."

"But not get nearly as much time and attention as she would if she were an only child," Gavin pointed out.

They looked at each other and sighed.

"Then there is the question of whether we choose a family right here in the community whom we already know as one of the three families to meet with Ava?"

"And risk their hurt feelings if we don't choose them in the end?" Gavin put another pot of coffee on.

Noting the baby beginning to stir, Violet went to the bassinet. "Or just stick with complete strangers?"

Watching his woman pick up the baby he also cared deeply about, Gavin felt a strange stirring in his heart. He pushed aside the unfamiliar emotion. Getting up to warm a bottle while Violet changed Ava's diaper, he forced his attention back to the task at hand. "Which carries another kind of liability entirely."

"Although," Violet noted, contentedly cuddling Ava close, "if Mitzy and social services has approved them, they've already passed the litmus test."

A reluctant silence fell.

"What do you say we each choose our top three picks, write them down and then see which ones match up?"

Violet nodded, a fleeting sadness in her eyes. "Sounds good."

Afterward, they looked at the slips of paper.

Two families matched up.

"What do you say we ask Mitzy to introduce Ava to the two families we both agreed upon, to start, and go from there?" Violet suggested.

Gavin nodded. "Sounds like a plan."

"I DIDN'T EXPECT to see you at the hospital today," Tara Warren said the following morning, when she ran into Violet in the staff lounge.

It was Gavin's turn to take care of Ava. Although he

wasn't exactly going it alone. His younger sister Bridgette had gone over to hang out and assist. "I've got a meeting with the chief of oncology."

"You're thinking of staying, then?" Tara asked hopefully.

"Through the New Year."

"I heard you were offered a position in San Antonio."

Violet nodded. News traveled fast. "I may have to turn it down, though, due to my personal obligations here."

"Ava?"

Another nod. Another stab to the heart.

"How is she doing?" Tara asked kindly.

"Great. Waking every two hours or so to eat and get a diaper change, then she goes right back to sleep."

Tara patted her rounded belly. "I can't wait until our little one is here."

Whereas Violet was dreading the day Ava left their lives. That was why she had to stop focusing on what was never going to be, and start dealing with what was within the realm of possibility. And that started with sitting down with her mentor.

"No question," Bart Remington said gruffly a short time later. "We want you here on staff, either full- or part-time. What we don't want is the uncertainty that comes with anything of a temporary nature. We need to know you're as committed to Laramie Community Hospital as LCH is to you." He cleared his throat. "So, if you can give us that, then great. If not, I suggest you go with a bigger organization—like the San Antonio job—where staff turnover is more easily absorbed and accepted."

"How long do I have to make my decision?"

"I want to know, one way or another, by the end of the week. Because if you're not going to be here, I'll need to line up someone who is willing to work part-time until Tara Warren goes on maternity leave and full-time after that."

"I'll let you know by then," Violet promised.

She thanked the chief and left, already having an idea what her decision was going to be. And it had nothing to do with the ramifications of her blossoming relationship with Gavin.

Or did it?

"So Nicholas lost everything?" Gavin repeated, dumbfounded.

Bridgette nodded. "Apparently he wasn't making enough quickly enough in the stocks he initially chose, so he decided to make a risky investment just before the stock cratered."

Gavin groaned. Had it paid off, of course, Nicholas would have been much better off financially. Since it hadn't… "How is he taking it?"

Bridgette continued feeding Ava. "He's embarrassed, of course."

Realizing he had let his family down again—by not noticing how distressed Nicholas was, and so not doing anything to prevent his little brother's rash actions—Gavin promised, "I'll make time to see him. Give him the support he obviously needs."

"Wait a few days," his sister advised, setting the bottle aside. "He needs time to deal with it on his own first."

Gavin watched as Bridgette placed Ava across her lap. "That's not the way you burp her," he told her.

Bridgette looked at him with the expertise of an NICU nurse. "I think I know how to do this," she said, gently patting Ava's back. A loud burp sounded.

Smiling victoriously, Bridgette shifted Ava and situated her to continue feeding her.

Unable to help himself, Gavin hovered over them. "That's not how she likes to be held, either," he said.

Bridgette sighed. Loudly.

Ignoring his sister's exasperation, Gavin gestured to

demonstrate what he meant. "Her head should be just a little bit higher, nestled against your bicep rather than just above the crook of your elbow, when she takes her bottle."

Bridgette rolled her eyes. "I *have* fed her before."

"When she was in the hospital," Gavin countered. "Things are different now."

His sister smiled tenderly at the little girl cuddled in her arms. "I should say they are."

Gavin frowned. "What is that supposed to mean?"

"You have baby fever." She winked. "Or should I say *Ava fever*?"

Gavin paced nearby, not sure when he'd felt so at a loss. "What's that supposed to mean?"

Ava began to fuss, just a little bit. He itched to take the infant in his arms again.

"Have you begun to reconsider your decision not to keep her?"

Gavin shook his head. "Violet and I agreed what was best at the outset. All our reasoning still stands."

"With one exception," Bridgette said, rising. She walked over to settle Ava in Gavin's arms. "The love you both obviously feel in your hearts."

Love?

He knew he loved Ava. Violet did, too. But wasn't the point of love to ignore your own selfish wishes and do what was best for the person you cared for?

After all, he loved his family dearly. But that didn't naturally make him an effective parent. If it had, he would have known what to say to Nicholas after the accident. He would have realized immediately how traumatizing the rollover was, and insisted Nicholas not go back to college right away. But instead, he'd let him go. Not having a clue that his little bro was so upset he was about to drop out of school. Or worse, gamble what remained of his tuition money away.

Bottom line, he had failed him. And thereby his whole family, again.

He couldn't fail Ava.

He could love her as a godparent. Care for her, watch over her.

But he could not be her parent.

Not without letting her down.

The question was, how would he explain this to Violet, in a way she would understand and accept. Gavin was still thinking about that long after Bridgette left.

When Violet returned, she had the ultra-determined cheerfulness about her that always meant more was going on with her than she wanted to admit. Which made sense, since more was going on with him, too.

Violet set down her keys and purse. She walked over to where he stood, a wide-awake Ava cradled in his arms.

"I saw Mitzy as I was leaving the hospital."

Uh-oh. Gavin did not like the sound of that.

Violet held out her hands.

Realizing what she wanted and needed, he shifted the baby to her.

Yet to burp, Ava blew out a tiny milk bubble between her rosebud lips. She turned her big eyes up to Violet.

She smiled down at Ava with what could only be interpreted as a mother's fierce and abiding love. Then turned back to Gavin, a hint of sadness in her eyes. "The visits between the first two sets of prospective parents are set up for ten o'clock tomorrow morning, in the visitation room at the family services center. Mitzy will be there the entire time, monitoring and recording the interactions for us to view later."

Aware she looked as anxious as he suddenly felt, Gavin reassured her, "I'm sure it will go smoothly."

"I know Mitzy will see that it does." Violet swallowed. "You're not working tonight, right?"

Gavin shook his head. "I'm off until midnight tomorrow."

"So we're both going to be here this evening?"

"Looks like. Unless you have errands or something you want to do."

"No. I'd just like to stay and enjoy what little time we have left with Ava."

"Sounds good to me," Gavin returned gruffly. It was the thought of her leaving, and of Violet maybe going away, too, as a consequence, that damn near broke his heart.

For a man without a romantic bone in his body, who would have thought?

OVER THE COURSE of the next twenty-four hours, Gavin and Violet shared taking care of Ava, made love several times and even managed to watch a DVD movie both had been wanting to see. And yet, even as things proceeded perfectly, Gavin could sense Violet slipping away from him.

It was as if to place Ava with another family, one much better suited to care for her than the two of them, she had to shut down part of her heart.

And while Gavin understood—he was having to compartmentalize his emotions, too, to get by—he worried her distance wouldn't end when this was over.

And that would be a problem.

For both of them.

Violet, however, didn't seem to realize that, as the morning of the prospective-family bonding sessions dawned.

She rushed around, doing everything that needed to be done and a lot that did not. "We should make a list. Shouldn't we make a list of her likes and dislikes?"

Gavin nodded, holding the infant so she, too, could watch Violet gather everything for Ava's very first tub bath. "Absolutely. These families shouldn't go in blind. They should have every advantage when it comes to bonding with Ava."

Violet knotted her hair on top of her head, then paused to kiss the baby's cheek. "That's what I think, too." Looking a lot more composed about the impending separation than he felt, Violet checked and then had him test the comfortably warm water in the baby bathtub that her sisters had loaned them, which was situated, along with several thick and fluffy bath towels, on the counter next to the kitchen sink.

Although the temperature outside had gotten cool overnight, the morning was warming fast. To ensure that Ava would stay warm enough, though, they had turned on the heat.

"What does the thermostat say?" Violet asked.

"Seventy-three, inside."

"That's good, don't you think?"

"Yep." They did not want the infant getting chilled when it came time for her very first tub bath.

With another quick efficient smile, Violet made sure she had everything ready. Gavin handed her over, staying close as Violet gently laid Ava on the towels and undressed her quickly.

"Okay, sweetheart." Violet cooed. "Here goes..." She cradled the baby's small body in one hand, her head and neck in the other, and then lifted her gently into the bath.

Ava's eyes widened in surprise.

Gavin wet a washcloth, as they had discussed, and placed it over the infant's chest to keep their little darling warm and calm.

And what do you know, Gavin mused, it worked. Violet smiled victoriously, too.

Together, talking softly, soothing all the while, he and Violet massaged a small amount of lavender-scented baby wash over Ava's hair and body, taking care to get the creases in her neck and arms and legs, and the area behind her ears.

An equally gentle rinse and she was done.

"Well, that wasn't so bad, was it?" Violet lifted the blinking infant out of the bathwater and into the thick, soft towel Gavin had waiting.

Gavin exchanged triumphant glances with Violet. "I thought we did great."

Maybe they were parent material, after all.

To the point they should be thinking about having one of their own one day.

When he and Violet could offer an infant everything he or she needed in life.

He snuggled Ava while Violet brought out the clothes. "The pink onesie or the yellow?"

Contentment rushed through Gavin as he cradled Ava tenderly in his arms. "Pink."

The baby blinked up at him. And was that a *smile*?

Violet was grinning happily now.

"Pink it is," she declared with the same tenderness Gavin was feeling.

Keeping Ava's top half covered, Violet diapered her, then removed the towel and slipped on an undershirt for extra warmth. The onesie followed. So did a cute little hat. And matching sweater. Unexpected tears misted Violet's eyes. "She looks…beautiful, don't you think?"

"Best. Baby. Ever," Gavin agreed hoarsely, barely able to get the words out.

Luckily, he had composed himself by the time they settled Ava into her carrier. Not daring to look at Violet, for fear if she were feeling as oversentimental as he was it would send him over the edge, Gavin hoisted the diaper bag over his shoulder. Violet fell into step beside him. Then they were out the door, in the car and on their way.

VIOLET KNEW SHE was doing the right thing. But it still felt as if someone had reached into her chest and yanked her heart right out.

"So what now?" Gavin asked after they had reluctantly handed Ava to the waiting social worker.

Violet couldn't help but note it seemed as though he was doing all he could to contain his emotions, too.

But letting their conflicted feelings affect Ava's future happiness would only make the situation all the more difficult when the time came to let her go. So, once again, Violet did what she had to do.

Calmly thrusting her hands into the pockets of her suede jacket, she walked with Gavin to her SUV. "I have to go out to McCabe House to check on the progress."

His gaze on the distant horizon, he asked, "Want company?"

More than he knew. "Sure," she said as if it was no big deal, when to her it was a *very* big deal.

Sterling had pushed her away when they had needed to be there for each other. It helped, having Gavin want her close instead.

The estate was quiet. Devoid of any other vehicles. Gavin frowned as she parked outside the stable-house. "Shouldn't the crews be here?"

Violet shook her head. "There's nothing for them to do right now. They're waiting on county inspectors to approve the structural changes made to date. I still need to check on things, too. Make sure there are no other broken pipes, or whatever."

When they entered McCabe House, there was nothing but a big, carved-out space on each of the two floors. All the drywall had been removed, the wood framing reconfigured.

Even the bathroom fixtures were gone. It was an open slate. And for Violet, who recalled visits to her grandparents when she was growing up, it was suddenly devastating to see.

Without warning, she burst into tears.

Alarmed, Gavin took her in his arms and held her close. "Hey," he said, stroking her hair. "Are you okay?"

No, she wasn't, and she didn't want to discuss why, so she offered the excuse that usually made men stop asking questions immediately. "Sorry. Hormones."

Maybe it was the fact he was a physician, or maybe it was the fact that he'd made love with her and slept with her wrapped in his arms, or spent hours taking care of a tiny little infant with her, but *whatever* it was that gave him superior knowledge about her, the end result was the same. Gavin wasn't buying it.

"You seemed fine this morning."

And last night, when they'd made love—twice—while Ava had slept. And cuddled after.

She blinked fiercely, willing away the moisture in her eyes, then rubbed at them, as if she had gotten some dust in them. "I probably just haven't had enough sleep." She waited until she had composed herself, lifted her head from his chest and shot him a look. "Neither of us has."

He studied her, apparently still thinking it was something else. Like, maybe, Ava, causing her to cry.

Not used to such scrutiny, Violet pushed away from him and strode out of the house. He followed her down the steps and across the yard to the stable-house. She walked inside, expecting to feel sanctuary.

Instead, as she looked around at the glamping setup that had once held such romance and promise, she felt another sucker punch to the gut.

Gavin curved a comforting hand over her shoulder. "What is it?"

Although her initial impulse was to push him away— again—Violet knew she needed to unburden herself, and she knew she could talk to him frankly, that he wouldn't judge her.

She turned on the ceiling fan and walked around, opening up the windows to let out the stale air. "A few weeks ago, I thought I had it all figured out. I was excited about taking the time off and being out here on my own." Whirling back toward him, she met his eyes and admitted, "I thought roughing it—"

"If you can call all this roughing it," he teased, working a laugh out of her despite her low mood.

"Okay," she corrected just as facetiously, "I thought glamping here would not only help my extended family and my grandparents' legacy, but clear my mind, help me figure out what the next step of my life should be. Instead, I've barely been out here the past couple of weeks."

"With good reason, given you were seeing to Ava."

Violet pushed her hands through her hair. "I've also reneged on my promise not to get too close to her."

He nodded, not arguing that. "I think we both have."

A contemplative silence fell.

"I no longer want the San Antonio job I worked so hard to get."

He shrugged, perching on the arm of the sofa. "So don't take it."

Violet paced closer, knowing, like it or not, this had to be said. "And most damning of all, I started a fling with you at the worst possible time."

He caught her as she passed and pulled her onto his lap. "Why is it the worst possible time?"

She splayed her hands across his hard chest. "Because I'm so confused!"

He rubbed his thumb across her lower lip. "Are you?"

She looked into his gray-blue eyes and saw the sexual intent. "What do you mean?"

His grin widened as he led her to what always made them both feel better. "I don't feel any confusion when you kiss me like this…"

Violet moaned and melted into him. "Gavin."

He cupped her breast. "Or I touch you, like this…"

Her nipple pearled against the center of his palm. Tingles of need swept through her.

He trailed kisses along the shell of her ear, down the nape of her neck. "Or you snuggle in my arms all night. Times like this—" he lifted his head to kiss her hard and long "—I think you know exactly what you want. Which just so happens—" he unbuttoned her blouse "—to be exactly what I want."

Violet snuggled close, her promise not to be distracted fading as the passion between them escalated. "And what's that?" she asked, cupping his face in both her hands.

His eyes grew shadowed; his voice, sexy-rough. "Time. Alone with you. Time to make love to you and hold you in my arms, and make love to you again and again and again."

So that's what they did.

Violet opened herself up to him, body and soul, and he took her with a masculine prowess that soon had her whimpering in pleasure. Blood rushed, hot and needy, through her veins. And then all was lost as they moved together toward a single goal, finding it, clinging to it, savoring the release. And in that instant Violet knew. She could really, really get used to having him in her life.

He held her tenderly. "So…still confused?"

The need on his face matched hers. "Not about wanting you," she whispered.

Rolling, so he was beneath her, she linked her arms around his neck. Kissed him sweetly. "I want you, too. In my bed, in my life."

And most of all, she thought wistfully, *in my heart.*

Chapter Fourteen

"So what do you think?" Mitzy asked later that afternoon, after they'd viewed the tapes.

Glad to have their young charge back in her arms, Violet observed, "Both couples seemed to interact well with Ava."

Gavin sent a fond look at the infant. "I thought so, too."

Mitzy made a few notes. "Which family strikes you as the family for Ava, though?"

Violet blinked, a little surprised by the pressure. "You expect us to make a decision *now*—based on one meeting?"

Mitzy's gaze narrowed with friendly rebuke. "It's not good for anyone involved to drag it out longer than necessary."

Violet stiffened. "I don't think we're dragging it out."

"We just don't have all the facts," Gavin said.

"Okay." Mitzy rocked back in her desk chair. "What else would you like to know? You have the financial statements of both families, the background checks, the statistics on how long and happily the couples have been married. Both also have large extended families in the area who have promised to care for Ava should anything happen to the parents before Ava is grown and on her own. Both have also agreed to allow you to be godparents and to see her as much as you wish. What else could you need to approve them?"

Violet looked at the split screen on the TV monitor,

where both prospective couples could be seen on tape, mooning over the baby. Ava was seemingly content with both.

"What else do you need to set your mind at ease?" Mitzy continued helpfully.

"I don't know. A crystal ball?" Violet said finally, only half jesting. "Some way of knowing whether we are making the right decision here. Or which couple we should choose." Because right now, even though both visits had gone admirably well, all she felt was unbearably sad and confused.

Gavin was brooding, too. "I think we'd be more comfortable if we had more time to consider this."

"I'm sure you would," the social worker said, her voice taking on a harder edge. She leaned forward, her forearms on the desktop, hands folded. "Unfortunately, the standard of care is not what's in the best interest for the two of you. It's what is in the best interest of the child. And that's to be placed with the couple who is going to raise her so that she can begin to bond with them before she gets any further attached to the two of you."

Mitzy paused to let her words sink in. "You can see that, can't you? That if this current arrangement continues, Ava will decide that you are her mommy and her daddy, and will make her preferences clear. In fact—" Mitzy nodded at Ava, who was clasping Violet's blouse with both tiny fists "—she may already be doing so. I have to say, she didn't physically cling to anyone else who held her today." Mitzy's observation brought a rush of heat to Violet's face. Was it possible, she wondered, that Ava had already decided she wanted *her* for a mommy?

She turned to Gavin to gauge if he felt the same. As usual, when the subject of Ava's permanent placement came up, his expression was maddeningly inscrutable.

"Bottom line, I need a decision from you two," Mitzy continued.

His outward cool fading, Gavin frowned. "You really expect us to decide today?"

The social worker nodded. "If you had to make a decision right this instant, which couple would it be?"

Silence fell as the pressure to let Ava go mounted.

Mitzy turned her head. "Violet?"

She swallowed, wanting to do her duty, but feeling more conflicted than ever. "I don't know." Her gut told her that both couples were completely right for Ava, and at the same time, totally wrong, too. Mostly because Ava didn't know them yet, at least not the way Ava knew her and Gavin.

"Gavin?" Mitzy prompted.

"I don't feel certain about either," he admitted with a shrug. "So maybe we should look at other couples."

Mitzy sighed her exasperation. "You already have. These are the two you selected, and the two who've met Ava and, by the way, completely fallen in love with her."

"Well, that's not hard to imagine," Violet grumbled, looking down at the baby nestled in her arms. Ava's expression was so completely trusting and content it almost broke her heart. "She is absolutely adorable."

"And in need of a *permanent* set of parents who love her," Mitzy said firmly. "*Now.* So go home and think about it, and get back to me first thing tomorrow morning."

Gavin gave Mitzy a challenging look. "Or what?"

She rose to show them out with cool determination. "The department and I will make the decision for you."

VIOLET WAS USED to making decisions under pressure. And feeling good about them. She did it all the time as an oncologist.

In either case the stakes were the same. Someone's life was in the balance.

So why was she having such a tough time now?

It wasn't as if she hadn't known this was what was going to happen all along. As Mitzy had said, the standard wasn't what was best for her and Gavin, it was what was in the best interest of the child. Still, something about the social worker's demand did not sit right with her. And she shared her feelings with Gavin the moment Ava had been put down to sleep.

"Mitzy is being unfair. We should at least have a few days to consider this."

Although Gavin had argued the same, in the social services office, in the short time that had passed, he seemed to have changed his mind. "Mitzy's right," he rumbled. "It's not going to get any easier for us to decide, and they need to know. So we need to deal with this and be done with it."

Done with Ava? Relegated to godparent status?

It was all Violet could do not to burst into tears. "Then *you* decide!" she retorted furiously. "Because I can't! Not with any certainty!"

Gavin's jaw set. He went into the kitchen and took out the coffee. "You're the emotionally intuitive one."

She lounged against the counter, *watching* as he filled the brewer with quick, economical motions and then switched it on. "That's just it, Gavin. As usual, I'm too emotional to be able to think straight."

"Then go with your instinct." Turning toward her, he pinned Violet with a hard stare. "What does your gut say?"

To keep her. And to share her upbringing with you.

But if Gavin wasn't willing…if it was going to be her as a single parent pitted against the possibility of a loving, married couple… Was that fair?

Violet shook off the dagger edge of guilt. And the

fiercer feelings of love that filled her heart whenever she was with the child.

She looked back at Gavin and said calmly, "Instinct is telling me to wait." *Until you know your own heart, too.*

Because, Violet thought, with a little more time, she was certain Gavin would reach the same conclusion she had come to. That the two of them should be in the running, too.

After all, Tammy had said in her videotaped will, Violet and Gavin didn't need to be married to be Ava's mom and dad. All they had to do was give Ava all the love in their hearts, which was considerable, and work together to raise her.

The fact that she and Gavin had proved they could live together under one roof, even in very small quarters, and were now friends—and lovers—well, that was an even bigger bonus. Because it portended well for their future as a "family," even if it wasn't a traditionally assembled one.

Unfortunately for all of them, Gavin did not appear to be thinking along the same lines.

As the smell of fresh-brewed coffee filled the small kitchen, he lounged opposite her, hands braced on the counter on either side of him. "You heard Mitzy. That's not an option. We have to pick one of them or social services will do it for us."

Hurt, confused and most of all scared she was going to make the wrong decision for all three of them, just the way she had once made the wrong decision when it came to her and Sterling's future, she threw up her hands and spun away. She set the papers, detailing all the information about the families, aside. "I still can't do it."

"Come on, Violet. We *have* to come to some conclusion."

"Then, as I said, if it's so easy, tough guy, you do it!"

Abruptly, he moved toward her and took her in his arms. Only this time the feel of his warm, strong body pressed against hers felt like an invasion, not a comfort. He tipped her chin up, forcing her to meet his gaze. "Why are you so angry at me?"

Because, Violet thought as a tidal wave of emotion swirled through her, *you don't feel the same way I do. You're not rushing to say this is all wrong. That you've changed your mind. That Ava doesn't belong with anyone else, she belongs with us.*

Because I can't understand how you can even consider giving our little baby girl—and I feel like she is our little baby girl in so many ways—over to strangers to raise. Especially after all we have been through.

And yet I feel incredibly selfish, too.

Am I acting in the best interest of the child?

And if I'm not, what does that say about me as a potential mother, that I would put my own heart and well-being ahead of the child I swear that I love?

Aware he was still waiting for an explanation, Violet sighed. "I *am* angry with you—with everyone and everything really—because I think that you and Mitzy are pushing me into a situation I don't want to be in." *The same way I once trapped Sterling into an engagement.* "And are trying to make this quandary a lot simpler than it is."

He stroked a comforting hand down her spine. "It is simple. Ava needs to be with the people who are going to raise her. We have two excellent options. We just have to pick one."

And then walk away.

The lump of misery in her throat tightened. It was all Violet could do to push the next sentence out.

She splayed her hands across his chest. "That means we're back to square one. Which parents do we choose?"

Gavin shrugged, his confusion mounting as surely as hers. "To be honest, much as I tried, I couldn't find anything even the tiniest bit disqualifying about either of them."

Fresh anger surged. She shoved at his chest. "That's no help."

"I agree. It isn't." He released her and moved away. Pausing, he poured two cups of coffee. "So maybe we should do the smart thing," he suggested finally, pushing the beverage into her hand. "Let Mitzy and the rest of the department decide. They're not so emotionally entangled. And they have a lot more experience than us in this kind of thing."

VIOLET LOOKED AT Gavin as if she knew he was right. At least on an intellectual level.

Drawing on every bit of practicality he possessed, Gavin tried to reassure her they were doing the right thing. "Either couple will give Ava the kind of secure, loving upbringing Tammy would have wanted for her little girl. And since it's going to be an open adoption, and we are still going to be her godparents, we'll be able to watch over Ava. You know Mitzy and the rest of the department will do so, too."

Everything he said made perfect, rational sense. So why, he wondered, was he suddenly having doubts about what they were doing?

He'd never been a baby person.

Never particularly wanted a family of his own.

But now that he'd been with Violet and Ava, he was beginning to wonder how he'd manage *without* a wife and kids. And how crazy was that, especially for a guy without a romantic bone in his body?

Abruptly, Violet seemed to shake off the emotions that had threatened to overwhelm her. "You're right," she said quietly, the determination he loved about her resurging even as her slender shoulders slumped. She stirred vanilla-flavored creamer into her coffee and took a tiny sip. "This was our original agreement, after all. That we'd step in only as long as need be and then see Ava off to a loving mom and dad with a solid, mapped-out future. And let's face it, Gavin, as much as we both care about her, and I know we both do care about her—"

"Yes," he interjected, his heart wrenching in his chest, "we do."

"We can't give her all that," Violet admitted reluctantly.

Yet, Gavin thought, wondering where that emotion had come from.

Lifting her chin, Violet gathered steam. "It's not fair to ask Ava to wait for us to figure everything out, and come up with a way we could make this all work on a long-term basis. *If* we could even do that, given the fact we've just recently hooked up." She sighed. "Ava has already suffered enough turmoil in her young life. She had a traumatic entry into the world and lost her birth mother in the process. She had to struggle just to survive."

"The little darlin' sure has been through quite an ordeal," he agreed.

"So, after everything she's gone through, she deserves a *real* home," Violet went on softly. "Two parents with a stable, loving marriage to serve as a solid family foundation." She shook her head in regret even as her eyes grew moist. "It would be selfish for us to keep her, given the fact that neither of us can compete with that, much as we might wish to do so."

She was finally seeing reason again, Gavin noted. So why wasn't he more relieved?

"You want to call Mitzy?" he asked in a rusty-sounding voice.

Reluctantly, Violet nodded. "Yes, I'll do it first thing tomorrow."

Aware she sounded as if her heart was breaking as much as his was, Gavin swallowed against the rising lump in his throat. He set his coffee aside and reached to take Violet's

hand. "In the meantime, we'll have one last evening together, at least before I head to the hospital at midnight,
to take my shift." *An opportunity for the three of us to say
a bittersweet goodbye.*

"Actually, Gavin…" Violet surprised him by ducking
his grasp. Pivoting, she collected her handbag and keys.
"I have to go to the hospital."

Gavin blinked. "Now?"

Nodding, she took one last gulp of coffee, then headed
for the door. "If I'm not going to be caring for Ava, I've
really got to go back to work. Pronto."

Whoa. Wait. He caught up with her at the door. "Where?"

One hand still on the doorknob, she rose and kissed
him lightly on the lips. "Where I belong." She gazed into
his eyes, letting him know with a long, lingering look that
although their temporary parenting stint was nearly over,
as they had known from the get-go that it would be, their
love affair with each other was not. "Where my future is.
Here in Laramie. With you."

Chapter Fifteen

"I have to be honest with you," Gavin told Ava a half an hour later when she woke for her feeding. "This isn't exactly the way I saw the evening unfolding."

He laid her gently on the waterproof pad and went about changing her diaper. "I figured the three of us would spend the evening together. Sort of a last hurrah doing all the things you like best. Hanging with the two of us, drinking milk. Maybe even take a buggy ride through the neighborhood for old time's sake—" he sucked in a breath, feeling an unfamiliar stabbing sensation in his chest "—before we take you to Mitzy tomorrow."

But that had not happened.

And now he and Violet would be tag-teaming Ava's care this evening.

Unless she got back to the house well before he had to leave for his shift.

Ava kicked her legs.

"Not that I blame Violet for running off to take a time-out and pull herself together. Doing what is right for you is hard on her. Heck, it's hard on me, too. But that's the responsibility we were charged with when we became your temporary guardians."

Finished, he shifted the little girl into his arms and offered her the bottle he had prepared for her when she had first started to stir.

Which, coincidentally, had been the moment Violet had exited.

"And it's a responsibility we take very seriously." He paused when Ava started to sip then moved her face away from the nipple.

"One day, when you're settled with your new family, you'll appreciate the sacrifice we've made."

A sacrifice that was already killing him inside. And they hadn't even done what was right yet.

Gavin shifted the baby a little higher in his arms.

He tried again.

Ava started to suckle, then stopped. Her tiny face scrunched up. She let out an indignant cry.

Panicking—had the baby warmer made the formula too hot?—Gavin hastily turned the bottle upside down and sprinkled milk on the inside of his forearm. It was lukewarm—just as when he had tested it.

So that wasn't it.

It had been freshly mixed with bottled water, too. Out of the same big can of powdered formula they had been using the past few days.

He carried Ava over and poured a little of the water he had used into a glass. Sipped. That was fine, too. Nothing out of the ordinary there. He taste-tested the powdered formula. Bland but okay.

Reassuring himself that it wasn't him she was rejecting, he took Ava back into the living room and settled in the rocking chair. "Maybe I wasn't holding you just right. Let's give this another try."

He settled her into the curve of his arm, making sure he had her head higher than her body, her neck nestled comfortably. He offered her the bottle. Ava grabbed it with both hands. This time she was able to take about four greedy sips without a problem.

He relaxed.

She drank on. Then abruptly let out a startled cry and arched her back slightly.

Another loud, indignant wail escaped her lips.

No problem with her lungs, the physician in him noted.

In fact, he had never heard her so ticked off, the daddy in him agreed.

"Do you have air in your tummy, is that it?" Determined to figure out what the problem was, he moved her to his shoulder. "Let's see if we can get you to burp."

Instead, all she did was cry, even more plaintively.

Gavin stood and began to pace. Calmly, he went down the checklist. Her diaper was fine.

She wasn't tucking up her legs, the way she would if she had colic.

But she was clearly unhappy about something. And definitely looking around at her surroundings.

For Violet?

It seemed so, but all the scientific studies said she was too young to have formed an emotional attachment to any one person.

Which meant it had to be something else.

"I'm not sure what is bothering you, sweetheart, but I know this. Violet will help me figure out what to do when she gets home in a little while."

Ava looked at him and wailed louder.

It was almost as if she sensed something was up.

But that was impossible. "You can't possibly have understood anything Violet and I were talking about today," he told her gently, still walking her back and forth, and cuddling her close. "So you don't know you're going to your forever home tomorrow, either," he said, his voice catching in his throat. He pushed the raw emotion aside and forced himself to be as strong as their little darlin' needed him to be right now.

Cradling her tenderly, he continued soothing—and

reassuring—her. "To a family that will flat-out adore you every bit as much as Violet and I do, if not more."

Ava abruptly stopped crying.

She looked at him with tear-filled eyes.

Regret welled within him. His resolve wavered. But with effort, he pushed his guilt aside. *Again.* It didn't matter what he wanted. What he wished. He knew, with every practical iota of his being, that he was doing the right thing in giving her to a set of parents far better equipped to raise her than he and Violet were.

He had to be strong.

Just as Violet was.

Had to do what was best for Ava. She turned away from him and began to cry again, even more poignantly. And what she needed now, he noted, was the kind of deeply intuitive, familial support he had never been able to give.

"You couldn't have picked a better time to come back," Tara told Violet when the two of them ran into each other in the hall just after 9:00 p.m. "One of your patients just checked in to the hospital."

"Carlson Willoughby?"

The oncologist nodded. "He's having surgery early tomorrow morning. I was going to go over the post-op treatment plan with him and his wife now. If you'd like to tag along…"

Violet knew the boundaries that had been put in place needed to be maintained. "I don't want to undermine you."

"You won't," Tara replied with confidence. "He has a brand-new attitude, thanks to the talk you had with him and his wife."

"One that was long overdue," Violet admitted, still feeling a little chagrined over her part in the untenable situation that had evolved.

"Well, whatever you said to him worked. Because he and Mrs. W. said they had faith in the entire medical center, and that included me. So however I want to proceed is fine with them."

Together, they walked toward the nurses' station. "Wow, that *is* a change."

Tara paused to pick up a chart. "I'd still like your input, though. Since you know the patient's response to former protocols better than anyone."

"I'd be glad to help out." Violet paused as the newly minted mom in her went on high alert. In the distance, an infant could be heard crying hysterically. It sounded an awful lot like Ava. In fact, Violet noted in alarm as she swung around to see Gavin striding toward her, a bawling Ava in his arms, it *was* Ava! Leery of further disturbing other patients on the floor, the two of them ducked into the nearby staff lounge.

Luckily, at that moment, it was quiet and empty.

Violet switched from doctor to mom mode in an instant. "What's wrong?" she said, instinctively holding out her arms.

His face taut with concern, Gavin handed the little girl over. "I think she misses you."

Violet wanted to say that was impossible. Ava was several weeks away from attaching to anyone in particular. Yet the moment they were together again, Ava stopped crying, blinked through her tears and looked up at Violet as if she had just saved the day.

A mixture of maternal tenderness and contentment swept through Violet.

"What's this all about?" she soothed, snuggling Ava close. "Why are you giving your da—" She almost said *daddy*, then stopped and corrected herself. "Um…Gavin, such a hard time?"

Another blink of Ava's dark lashes. A wince. And then a wail of complete and utter distress. This time she didn't stop. No matter what Violet said or did.

"How long has she been like this?" Violet asked, patting her back gently. Still Ava sobbed, her tiny fists clutching at Violet's white coat until Violet thought her own heart would break.

"It started off and on as soon as you left the house."

Which had been three hours ago, Violet noted.

"It's only been the past forty minutes or so that I couldn't get her to stop crying at all." His eyes narrowed. "I checked everything. Her diaper's dry. I fed her—or tried to. I held her upright so she could burp—which she did with no problem."

"Did you try swaddling her?"

Gavin raked a hand through his dark hair. "And de-swaddling. Nothing worked." He paused, broad shoulders tensing. "What now?"

"I'm not sure." Her concern mounting, Violet looked at Gavin. "But maybe we should have her checked out. Who is the pediatrician on call tonight?"

He pulled up the schedule on his phone. "Your mom."

With a hiccup, Ava abruptly stopped crying.

Gavin studied the infant in relief.

Exhausted, Ava laid her head on Violet's chest.

Love swelled in Violet's heart. She knew she wasn't the baby's mother, but she certainly felt like it. Tenderly, she touched her hand to Ava's cheek. It was wet with tears but not warm enough to indicate fever. Still… "We might be overreacting here, but to play it safe, I think I'm going to ask my mom to take a look at her."

Gavin paused, brow furrowed. "You really think there is something wrong with Ava—other than simply missing you tonight?" Beneath the worry in his tone there was something else she could not immediately identify. Something nearly as unsettling.

Violet looked him in the eye, nodded. "And deep down you do, too. Otherwise you wouldn't have rushed her to the hospital to see me."

FIFTEEN MINUTES LATER Violet sat on a gurney in an exam room, holding Ava tenderly in her arms, while her mother went through the physical exam. Gavin stood nearby, watching with concern, ready to help in any way needed.

"It's an ear infection," Lacey McCabe said after viewing Ava's ear canal with an otoscope. "It's just starting, but it looks to be painful. We'll start Ava on acetaminophen and an antibiotic right away. She'll be feeling better in no time."

"Thanks, Mom." Teary with relief, Violet cuddled Ava close while Gavin zipped up her sleeper.

Lacey McCabe shot a tender look at the patient, then paused to write out the orders. "No problem." She ripped off the prescription and handed it to Gavin, who was suddenly struggling to contain his emotions, too.

"I was going to ask if you had decided on a family for Ava yet." Lacey looked from the baby to Violet to Gavin, and back to her daughter again with maternal wisdom. "And maybe you have?"

It wasn't a question Violet had expected. Yet she knew the answer with a certainty as solid and real as this moment in time. An answer that had been coming for a while now. She had just been afraid to admit it out of fear that, as in the past, the happiness she yearned for would not materialize, after all.

A lump in her throat, she nodded slowly.

Her mother hugged her, suddenly a little teary-eyed, too. "Oh, honey," Lacey said thickly. "I thought this might be the case. And for the record…I think you're doing the right thing."

"WHAT WAS ALL that about with your mom tonight?" Gavin asked after they'd picked up the medicine at the hospital pharmacy and driven the short distance home.

Violet lifted Ava from her car seat and carried her inside the house. The trauma of the evening had worn the little one out. Now that the acetaminophen had taken effect, she was once again sleeping soundly. "My mom just figured out I'm going to adopt Ava," she said, a remarkable calm coming over her.

And now that she'd made the decision, she was suddenly feeling so much better! As if this was where they had all been headed, after all. Soon, Gavin would have to admit it, too.

Eyes narrowed, Gavin closed the door behind him. "This isn't what we discussed earlier this evening."

How well Violet knew that. She had almost made the worst mistake of her life. And all because she had refused to listen to what her heart was telling her. Gently, she lowered Ava into the bassinet. To her relief, the exhausted infant kept right on sleeping.

She walked into the kitchen, staying close enough to keep an eye on the baby yet far enough away that their conversation wouldn't wake her.

Violet leaned against the counter, aware Gavin hadn't come to his senses yet. But that was okay, she could help him get there.

She looked up at him. "Earlier this evening I thought the same you did, that everything had to be perfectly worked out for Ava to be happy." She shook her head, her heart clenching at the grave mistake that had almost been made. "But I didn't understand that what she really needed was to be with us." Her heart filling with joy, Violet sent another tender glance the baby's way. "But she showed us how wrong we were."

Gavin came closer, appearing as sure of himself as he

was in the ER every day. "Look, I know this evening was traumatic for you and for Ava. It was hard on me, too," he said calmly. "But that's no reason to let our overwrought emotions drive us to do something ill-advised."

Violet straightened to her full height. "Tell me you're not comparing what I'm about to do to the fact your brother dropped out of college after his accident!"

He kept his dark gaze locked with hers. "Our situation is more complicated than that."

You think? "Well, at least we agree on something!" Violet fired back.

"However, the underlying principle remains the same," he went on reasonably, suggesting she would soon come to the same conclusion. "Never make major decisions in the wake of a potentially life-altering event."

Aware she suddenly felt so shaky she could barely stand, Violet tucked her arms against her chest to still their trembling. "So you don't love Ava," she choked out, an unbearable sadness coming over her.

Abruptly, Gavin looked as irked as she felt. "Of course I love her," he said gruffly. "It's impossible to be around her and not love her. She's a great little kid. Sweet and adorable. Her effervescent personality shines through even at this young age."

So what was really happening here?

Why weren't they on the same page with this when they were so close in so many other ways? Violet gestured in confusion. "Then?"

Gavin released a frustrated breath. "I want her to have everything she deserves."

Still struggling to understand where he was coming from, Violet pushed on. "Including?"

"Two parents who don't panic when something goes wrong."

Was that it? Violet wondered in a mixture of frustration and relief. Gavin thought he had failed Ava? Failed them both? The same way he felt he had oft let down his family? It hardly mattered as long as one of them had remained calm, and Violet had. "Yes, but I didn't panic," she reminded him quietly, looking him right in the eye.

His jaw tautened. "*I* did."

Violet took his big hand in hers. "And that's normal for new parents," she reassured him softly. "My mom told us that when we had the whole can't-get-her-to-sleep-in-anything-but-our-arms debacle, when we first brought Ava home from the hospital."

He averted his gaze and moved away from her. Getting a glass from the cabinet, he poured himself some water from the tap. "You know what Tammy's request was."

Violet joined him at the sink. She tipped her head back to better see his face. It was all she could do to keep her voice from rising. "I know what Tammy's ideal outcome was. That you be Ava's daddy and I be her mommy. And see that she has lots of extended family so she'll always have someone to love her, no matter what." And now that Violet had come to her senses, she fully intended to do just that.

Gavin stared at her in weary resignation, then spread his hands wide, reminding her tersely, "And if that didn't work out, which Tammy fully expected it might not, she wanted us to find a local family to love her baby girl. Arrange for an open adoption and be Ava's godparents. And you and I agreed from the outset, when we went over all the options—" he set the glass down with a thud "—that the last scenario was best."

"That was before we got so involved with her and each other," she told him thickly.

Noting he had a little spit-up on his shirt, he strode into the bedroom. Tugged that and his T-shirt, which was similarly soiled, over his head. He dropped both onto the basket on top of the washer and then headed, bare-chested, to his closet for a new one.

Violet followed, taking in the masculine set of his broad shoulders and taut abs.

She wished she could fall into his arms and make love with him, and let all their problems fall away, but she also knew that would only be avoiding the inevitable.

She lounged against the dresser, watching him get ready for his shift, which would start in less than thirty minutes. Taking a deep breath, she looked him in the eye. "That was before I understood what it was to love a child so completely. Or to have a baby look to me as her mommy." Violet stared at the hard, aloof expression on his face, wondering how everything could be falling apart so fast.

Desperately, she tried again. "Ava wanted me tonight, Gavin." She beseeched him to understand. "And when you're with her, and she's not trying to communicate that she has an earache, she wants you, too."

Gavin brushed his teeth and splashed water on his face and then dried his face with a towel. He swung back to face her, his expression all the more intent. "Ava also enjoyed being with Mitzy and both sets of adoptive parents. She snuggles up to my sister and all the nurses from the Special Care Nursery at the hospital, too."

Unable to dispute the truth, Violet fell silent.

He folded his arms across his chest. "Listen to me, Violet. We have to take a step back here and look at the situation realistically. We have to honor our promise to do what is best for Ava, not just in the present but in the long run."

That was gut-wrenchingly similar to what Sterling had said to her when he hadn't wanted to marry her, after all, Violet noted miserably.

"Adopting her together may be what is best for you, and maybe even me, but it isn't what's best for Ava." Eyes serious, Gavin paused to let his words sink in. "We can't make rash decisions based on ER emotion."

Frustrated that he wouldn't let himself feel what she did for the child in their care, Violet countered with equal certitude. "The Willoughbys did. They met in an ER, decided there was something there and got married a week later. And they're still together some sixty years later. Still passionately in love with each other, even as they work together to battle Carlson's cancer."

Gavin stood his ground. "And a lot of others who did the very same thing got divorced." He headed for the fridge and took out the makings for a sandwich. "We made our decision earlier this evening. Had Ava not developed an ear infection, that decision would still stand."

She watched him layer thinly cut ham and Swiss cheese on oatmeal bread, and finish it off with a slathering of brown mustard. Methodically, he began putting together a meal.

"So once again fate intervenes!" She stepped back so he could get a sandwich bag from the drawer. "Don't you get it? The universe is trying to tell us something and we need to pay attention to what that is!"

He dropped the sandwich and an apple into a brown paper bag, closed the top and set it aside. He exhaled roughly, looking as ticked off as she felt. "You're being hopelessly idealistic. You know that, don't you?"

She glared in exasperation. They didn't have time to argue the point; he had to be at the hospital in fifteen minutes. "And you're being ridiculously pragmatic! Maybe because you don't really want to commit fully to anyone. Not to an ex-fiancé, not to Ava, not to me…"

A stressful silence fell.

Aware she was on a roll, she continued, "Because as long as you use your past insufficiencies where your loved ones are concerned as an excuse, you'll never risk it all with anyone else. You'll never risk being hurt, the way you're hurting me. And Ava. And anyone else who dares to love you."

"You don't mean that," he countered brusquely.

Didn't she?

As they stared at each other Violet wondered if she had ever really known him at all. Or had she just seen what she had needed to see and felt what she had wanted to feel to justify their reckless affair?

There was only one thing she knew for certain. Only one thing she had to hang on to, as she warned, "I'm not letting Ava go, Gavin. I've made up my mind about that. And Ava and I are a package deal."

Gavin's jaw hardened. He looked at her, a world of hurt and disappointment in his eyes. "What is that supposed to mean?"

Violet threw up her hands and moved farther away from him. "If you don't want to do this, then that's your right," she vowed, hot, bitter tears pressing against the backs of her eyes.

Even though the thought of him walking away from their little girl—and Ava *had* become their little girl in the past few weeks—crushed her heart and soul.

"But I can't—and won't—put Ava in the position of being around someone who doesn't love her the way she deserves." The way Sterling had dissed her. "Because you're right," she said shakily, pointing to the bassinet. "That little girl sleeping in there? She commands only the best."

Gavin stared at Violet as if he couldn't believe it had actually come to this. "You're leaving me?" he asked hoarsely.

Violet nodded, knowing it was the right thing, too. She swallowed around the lump in her throat and ran a weary hand through her hair. "Turns out I need someone with a romantic bone in his body, after all."

Chapter Sixteen

Gavin punched in the security code and walked in the back. Closed for business as always on Sunday, the Monroe family store was devoid of customers, the only sound the ripping open of shipping boxes.

His younger brother turned to face him. "What are you doing here?" Nicholas asked Gavin.

Fulfilling my obligation as your family. "Thought you might need a hand setting out the new inventory," Gavin said.

Nicholas gave him an assessing look. "That bad, huh?"

"What?"

Nicholas went over to turn on the sound system. "Your life—since Violet broke up with you."

Gavin frowned. "She didn't break up with me."

Nicholas dipped his head in acknowledgment as he did a little two-step to the beat, then went back to unpacking the new inventory. "That's right. You were never *officially* a couple."

It had sure felt that way, Gavin thought.

"Just co-guardians to that baby girl." Nicholas entered the details of the shipment into the store computer.

That baby girl had a name. And the most winsome face and incredibly innocent and trusting blue eyes...

"Ava," Gavin corrected, his heart melting a little whenever he thought of his soon-to-be-goddaughter.

Nicholas tilted his head. "So you miss her, too? Not just Violet?"

More than he wished to admit. Reminding himself he was still doing what was best for Ava, however, Gavin shrugged. "I saw her yesterday when I went to visit her." *And Violet was at the hospital, working.*

Nicholas punched a few more numbers into the computer. "Bridgette said you showed up while she was babysitting." He paused sympathetically. "And that you looked like you had lost your best friend and your dog and your truck, all in one really bad day."

The last thing Gavin wanted to do was to compare his life to the lyrics of some sad song.

Although he felt devastated by the way things had turned out, no question. Violet had said she would stand by him, even after they gave the baby up. She hadn't.

Nicholas grabbed a stack of price tags. "Although," he added consolingly, "Bridgette said little Ava seemed *really* happy to see you."

She had been, Gavin remembered tenderly. Cuddling close, fisting her little hands in his shirt and looking up at him with those guileless blue eyes, seeming to say to him that it wasn't too late, this could all still be fixed. Violet's deliberate absence during his visit, however, had said otherwise.

Gavin pushed the foolish burst of hope away, figuring what was done was done.

If Violet said it was over, it was.

"I'm not here to talk about me," he told his little brother quietly. "I just wanted to let you know that if you need anything, I'm here for you."

"I know that." Nicholas sobered. "You always have been." Before Gavin could interrupt, Nicholas lifted a hand. "I just didn't always want you to be there for me.

I wanted to grow up. Make my own mistakes. Be on my own a little, you know?"

Gavin did.

"Figured out what you're going to do next?"

Nicholas attached price tags to the shirts. "Now that I lost all my recouped tuition money in day trading?"

Gavin nodded, seeing no need to sugarcoat things, either. "I'll loan you what you need to go back to school next semester."

"Thanks." Nicholas handed him an attachment gun, a stack of price tags and shirts. "But I want to work my way through school this time."

His little brother had grown up. "Are you sure?" Gavin asked.

Nicholas carried a stack of tagged clothing to the shelf. "Look, I know that you think that I did all that stuff because of the accident."

"Because I wasn't there for you after the trauma the way I should have been," Gavin agreed.

"But the truth is I had been thinking about dropping out of school all summer, just skipping ahead to a career, the way Michael Dell and Steve Jobs did. I figured I'd make a few really smart investments in the stock market and then I'd be well on my way to becoming the next Mark Cuban."

Now it all made sense. "Only, it didn't happen that way," Gavin concluded.

Nicholas went back to pricing. "And you know what the worst part of all of it is? I was squandering my chances long before that. Because even though I had this great opportunity to make something more of my life while I was at UT, I was never all in."

Gavin paused. "What do you mean? You were a great student. On the Dean's List from first semester on."

"Trouble is," Nicholas told him bluntly, "I didn't really

do anything my first year and a half there except focus on my class work."

Gavin continued to defend his little brother's choices. "You had a social life. Friends..."

"Yeah, but I never committed myself to having the whole university experience. I barely went to any sporting events, never joined any clubs or causes, or went to any of the guest lectures or interesting exhibits on campus. Instead, I lived in the same small-town-kid cocoon I grew up in, passed on the opportunity to meet a lot of new people and hung with the same kids." His frown deepened. "All the while resenting the fact that my life in Austin wasn't nearly the adventure I had expected it to be."

He shook his head in regret and looked Gavin right in the eye. "The point is, big brother, I could have had everything I wanted or needed *if only* I had seen the value of what was right in front of me. And you know what?" Nicholas paused, suddenly looking older than his years. "You could, too."

"DECIDE YET WHERE you're going to live now?" Poppy asked Violet early Tuesday morning when the two of them met at McCabe House, to begin packing up Violet's belongings.

She cast a look at the baby buggy parked in a quiet corner of the stable-house. Ava was inside, fast asleep. But she wouldn't stay that way for long, so Violet had to get busy. She went back to the wardrobe boxes she'd brought out and began to fill them for later transport. "Ava and I looked at two rentals yesterday when I got off work."

"And?"

"Both were fine. In town, close to both the hospital and Mom and Dad's place. I'm not sure I want to live in an apartment with a baby, though—and that's all that was readily available. Too much potential for noise from other neighbors. And what if Ava wants to go outside?"

"I don't know." Poppy pressed an index finger against

her cheek and pretended to think. "You go to a park? Or over to Mom and Dad's? Or my place?"

Violet rolled her eyes at the droll suggestion. "You forgot Rose and Lily." Her triplet sisters. "And Maggie and Callie." The twins, who lived in San Antonio. "They all live on ranches."

Poppy grinned. "It would be a little far to go for a twenty-minute romp in the grass, I suppose. Although having Ava play with her cousins would be nice."

Violet smiled, imagining just that. "It will be."

"Do you have any other options?"

Violet packed quickly. "Mom and Dad's, where we are residing now."

"What about the place where you were bunking when you first brought Ava home from the hospital?"

Nice way to bring the subject around to her failed romance.

Violet made a comical face at her sister. "Cozy as that would be, I really can't see me kicking Gavin out of his home."

Poppy waggled her brows mischievously. "Why should he have to leave?"

Violet groaned.

"He loves Ava, too," Poppy pointed out.

"Not enough to adopt her."

Her sister—who'd recently had great success convincing her best male friend to adopt a child with her, sans romance, sans marriage—waved off the small detail. "Give the man time."

Violet wished.

Disappointment spiraling through her, she reminded her sister, "We didn't have time. Mitzy wanted a decision within twenty-four hours. After some initial confusion about what was the best thing to do, I finally figured out what really matters in this world—"

"Loving someone and having them love you back?"

Violet nodded. "I told Gavin what I wanted us to do. Unfortunately, he disagreed."

Another shrug. "So he made a mistake."

If only he would admit that! Our lives would be so very different. But he hadn't, so...

"He knows his own mind, Poppy."

"True enough. But does he know his own heart?"

Good question, Violet thought as a melancholy silence fell. Not that it mattered now.

Determined not to make the same slew of mistakes she had before, Violet taped the moving box shut with a vengeance. "I can't pretend I know better than Gavin what he wants and needs, Poppy."

Poppy's eyebrows rose. "Even if you do?"

Violet focused on the packing. "I can give Ava all the love she needs, as a single parent. Plus, I'll have the entire McCabe clan as backup."

Poppy hung clothes inside another wardrobe container. "Sounds good."

Another silence.

Violet read her sister's mind. "But still less than ideal."

"You've always been all about striving for perfection."

Didn't she know that, Violet thought ruefully, striding past the Conestoga wagon, where she and Gavin had first slept together and later made love.

"And up to now, that's never really worked out." She could admit that now. Admit she had been holding on to an ideal that was never going to happen, and circumventing her own potential happiness in the meantime.

Poppy came closer, planting her hands on her hips. "So *now* you're going to settle. Give up on Gavin—"

"Whoa there, Nellie." Violet held up a palm to stop her. "I never gave up on him. He gave up on us." *As a couple, as potential parents, as a family...*

"In what sounds like a rare moment of self-doubt."

It had been that, all right. Had Mitzy not been pressuring them to make a decision…had Ava not had an ear infection…had Gavin, one of the best ER docs around, not missed it…would the result have been the same?

After all, before Ava had gotten sick, Violet had been ready to relinquish her care out of a misguided sense of nobility, too. Because she had thought the only way she could really honor the task she had been charged with—the only way Ava would be happy—was if she were in a traditional family, with a mother and father who were happily married and had been for a while.

She hadn't taken into consideration Ava's closeness with her, or Gavin, or the fact the three of them had already bonded, irrevocably. She hadn't taken into consideration the love she felt. Was it possible Gavin felt that same level of affection, and just would not—could not—admit it to himself, for the very same reasons that had almost stopped her?

"It was a mistake to let things end between you and Gavin like that. You must know that," Poppy persisted.

She did, and she didn't, Violet thought.

On the one hand, she still wanted to be with Gavin more than life.

On the other…she couldn't shake the nagging sense of déjà vu, or the worry that she was once again in an untenable situation, chasing after a man in the wrong way, at the wrong time.

She wiped the tears from her eyes with the heels of her hands. "I can't force him to want to be with us," she said, her voice breaking.

Poppy engulfed Violet in a warm, sisterly hug. "Oh, honey," she murmured consolingly, as only a big sister could. "You don't have to." Poppy hugged her all the tighter. "Don't you know that?"

"THERE'S BEEN A SNAG in the process," Mitzy Martin told Violet later that same week.

Her heart skittering in alarm, Violet set the infant carrier on the floor of the social worker's office. Ava cooed softly, oblivious to all that was at stake. Determined to make this work, no matter what, Violet sat opposite Mitzy. Silently vowing that once she had the temporary guardianship made permanent, she could work on resolving the rest of her problems, starting with her broken relationship with Gavin.

"If you're worried about the potential noise factors in the apartments I was considering renting, you needn't be," Violet told the social worker, aware that now that her mind was made up she was more optimistic than she had been in a long time. "I decided to take my parents up on their offer to have us bunk with them for a while."

Their large Victorian wasn't exactly the cozy domain Gavin's home had been, but it would do, for now.

Mitzy straightened the stack of paperwork in front of her. "I'm glad your parents were able to convince you to do that. But that wasn't the problem."

Stymied, Violet asked, "Then what was?"

Mitzy looked toward the open doorway.

"Me," Gavin said simply.

He strolled in. Clad in a dove-gray shirt that brought out the stormy hue of his eyes, coordinating tie and jeans, hair clean and rumpled, he looked sexy and as masculine as could be. His manner both serious and genial, he locked eyes with Violet for a heart-stealing long moment; one that said he had missed her every bit as much as she had missed him the past few days. He then knelt to say hello to Ava.

The infant gurgled happily as she looked up at him.

He held out his hand. Ava curled her fingers around his finger and held on as tightly as Violet suddenly wished she could.

Mitzy looked on, as amicably inscrutable as always. "Let's get started, shall we?" she said mildly.

Gavin nodded. He kissed the back of Ava's hand, then gently extricated himself and put a soft cotton rattle in her fingers. Rising, he took a seat beside Violet and turned to look at her once again.

She swallowed nervously. This was *not* how her reunion with the handsome physician was supposed to go!

Before Violet knew it, she was pivoting toward him in her seat, so quickly her knees brushed the hard musculature of his thigh.

Tingling at the brief, sensual contact, she pulled back slightly, until they were no longer touching. "I thought you were okay with me adopting Ava on my own?" That was the word he'd sent her through Mitzy, anyway.

His expression solemn, Gavin admitted, "Before I'd had time to really think about it, I thought that was Ava's best option."

"But now?" Violet urged. Her heart thundered in her chest. Her spirits rose and crashed and rose again.

Gavin looked more coolly determined than she had ever seen him. "Ava needs a mother *and* a father, Violet." He continued practically, before she could draw a breath. "She needs both of us."

Which, ironically, was what Violet had been saying for days now. Still, it took a moment for his gruff declaration to register. She stared at him in amazement. "You want to adopt her now, too?"

He nodded, all the love and commitment she had ever wanted to see shining in his eyes. "Along with you. Just as Tammy Barlowe wanted."

And what about the two of us? Violet couldn't help but wonder. *Do we take a step back? Pick up where we left off? Find some new way to carry on?*

His inscrutable expression gave no clue.

Violet knew what she wanted, of course.

But were they on the same page? Or would they differ here, too? And how would she feel if they did?

She only knew she wanted him back in her life, but for the right reasons this time. Reasons that were grounded in reality, not wishful thinking.

Seeming to understand they needed a moment alone, Mitzy stood and picked up the baby carrier. With an efficient smile, she announced, "Ava and I are going to give you a few minutes to talk. If you-all need us, we'll be down the hall saying hello to other members of the staff."

The door shut behind her.

The romantic, idealistic side of Violet wanted to throw herself into Gavin's arms then and there. The more practical side urged her to slow down this time and to proceed a hell of a lot more cautiously. That process started by understanding what was in his heart.

She stood and paced a safe distance away from him. "What changed your mind?"

His lips curved ruefully. "A number of things," he admitted in chagrin. Rising slowly, he kept his eyes on hers. "For starters, I realized you were right. I love Ava as my own, too."

She hitched in a shaky breath. Tears of joy and relief blurred her vision. She pushed the words around the lump in her throat. "Then why didn't you say so?"

His mouth tightening with regret, he said, "Because missing that diagnosis really shook me. I'd never had my emotions get in the way of being a doctor. Never mind expect it would happen as a father."

The pain in his low tone matched the anguish she'd felt in her heart.

Swallowing, Gavin shoved both hands through his hair. "To be perfectly honest, I wasn't sure I was good enough for her. Or for you. I've had a lot of loss in my life already, and you and I both know I don't exactly have the best track record where relationships are concerned."

With a rough breath, he closed the distance between them and took her hand. "I couldn't stand the thought of letting either of you down, and instead, that's exactly what I did. Even though I had promised, having been orphaned myself, that I would never turn my back on another parentless child."

Glad he was finally telling her all that was in his heart, she took his other hand and looked up at him. "What happened to make you feel differently?" Because clearly, a lot had changed. "What happened to help you understand that not only are you good enough for Ava and me, but exactly who we want and need?"

Affection lit the ruggedly handsome planes of his face. Briefly, he told her about the talk he'd had with his younger brother. "Turns out I'm more of a role model than I thought. And I had plenty of time to think, to miss her and miss you, and realize what my life would be like *with* the two of you in it, and what it would be like without." His grin widened. "You-all won, hands down."

Joy poured through Violet as Gavin took her all the way into his arms.

He pressed a kiss to her temple, her brow. Stroking a hand through her hair, he teased, "And you know what else I figured out?"

Her curiosity piqued, Violet put her arms around his waist. "Tell me."

"That you're right. Some decisions are best made on pure emotion. Like the first time I kissed you," he reflected fondly. "That was an impulse and a darn good one."

He paused to demonstrate, most effectively, she thought as tingles slid through her head to toe.

He rubbed his thumb across her lower lip. "Then there was the first time we slept together, the first time we made love. Hell," he corrected, chuckling mischievously, "*every* time we made love."

"No quarrel there."

His voice dropped another husky notch. "That was all done from what we both felt—in here." He touched both their hearts, in turn.

But there was a time, Violet noted, they needed to do things…his way, too.

"Still," Violet cautioned, stepping back and calling on her practical side, "there are some things we need to weigh and consider."

His eyes narrowed. "Such as?"

"How this is all going to work out."

"If you're asking me what I want, it's for you and Ava to move back in, pronto."

Violet swallowed. They were definitely headed in the right direction, but there was still no talk of love. And without that…would it work out? Could it work out? Long-term? "Isn't that how we got into trouble in the first place?" she asked, determined to put on the brakes, at least temporarily, before they derailed again. "By rushing into being a family?"

He shook his head. "No. We got into trouble when I stopped listening to my heart and almost convinced you to stop listening to yours and give Ava up." He exhaled slowly, all the regret he felt in his gaze. "I'm not going to make that same mistake again." He gathered her close. "I love you, Violet, with all my heart and soul."

Violet closed her eyes as she let the wonderful feeling sink in. Finally, she opened her eyes and kissed him. "Oh, Gavin," she breathed, "I love you, too. So very much." She didn't need more time to know that.

He pulled back to study her, even more serious now. "Enough to marry me?"

At last, the heartfelt proposal she had been waiting for

all her life. "You're sure?" she whispered tremulously, aware all her dreams were about to come true at long last.

He nodded. "Positive." He kissed her again, sweetly and tenderly, before flashing a mischievous grin. "Because as it turns out, I do have a romantic bone in my body, after all."

Epilogue

One year later

"Up!" Ava commanded with heartfelt urgency, holding out her arms to Gavin.

He flashed her an indulgent smile. "You got it, sweetheart." He swooped Ava into his arms and cradled her against his chest.

Smiling, the fourteen-month-old propped one elbow on his shoulder and used the other hand to crinkle the collar on his shirt between her fingertips. "Daddy," she announced affectionately.

"Ava," Gavin replied in turn, bussing the top of her head.

Ava beamed at the sound of her name, then turned to Violet and pointed. "Mommy," she declared happily.

Violet blew her a kiss. "My sweet, sweet baby girl."

Ava giggled, glad everyone had been properly identified, then squirmed to get down. "Play." She pointed toward the backyard. Together, the three of them walked outside.

Gavin lowered their little girl gently to the grass. Ava took a moment to get her balance before toddling over to her sandbox. Perching on the edge, she picked up her pail and shovel and began to awkwardly sift sand, a few grains at a time.

"So what do you think?" Gavin asked, turning the conversation to the new addition on their house.

Violet reflected on her decorator-sister's handiwork. It was gorgeous, down to the last detail of Ava's pink-and-white-gingham bedroom, the second bath and the cozy sunroom that opened up onto their backyard.

But then, that was no surprise. Poppy was a master at creating warm and inviting spaces.

"I think," Violet said softly, "I'm very glad that we elected to build on rather than move. This place has so many memories."

Keeping a watchful eye on their daughter, Gavin wrapped his arm around Violet's shoulders and tugged her close. "We brought Ava home from the hospital here."

Violet relaxed against him, savoring the masculine scent and feel of him. "This is where we got to really know each other and fell in love."

His eyes locked with hers. "And decided to formally adopt our little darling."

Which was, she thought, contentment filling her heart, one of the very best decisions of their entire lives. "It's where you officially presented me with an engagement ring."

He kissed the back of her hand. Then, looking every bit as satisfied as she felt, tilted her head up to his. "And we got married last spring."

Violet couldn't help but chuckle. "That was a day, all right."

Laughing, he shook his head. "We planned to have the ceremony outside."

She smoothed her hands across his chest. "And it rained."

He nodded, his hands slipping to the curve of her hips. "So we moved everything—and everyone—inside."

Warmth zinged through her. "To the point we barely had room to move."

His gray-blue eyes crinkled at the corners. "But it was incredibly special, anyway."

Wrapping her arms around his neck, Violet rose on tiptoe to kiss him. "As are all our moments."

Gavin hauled her even closer. He returned her kiss, thoroughly, tenderly. "And now that we have everything..." he murmured, brushing his lips across her temple.

"Ahh. More than you know," Violet whispered in return.

Gavin lifted a brow.

Violet blushed. She cast a look at their daughter, who was still happily playing in the sand. Violet had been planning to wait. But the news was too good not to share.

She swallowed and said, "We're expanding our family a little sooner than we had figured." Which probably wasn't a surprise given how often and passionately they made love.

Gavin's sexy smile widened slowly. "You're...?"

"Pregnant. Yes, Doc, I am."

The laugh erupted out of his chest, warm and exultant. "When?"

"If my calculations are correct, next May."

Violet shook her head. She waved her hand at the new construction. "So this addition we just spent the past six months building..."

His eyes twinkled. "May not be room enough. That's okay. Next time we'll just have to build up."

They were going to have to—otherwise they'd have zero backyard for their kids to play in.

"Always an adventure with us," she surmised.

Gavin hugged her close. "Good thing we're up to the task. Although, for the record, a second story would be nice."

They could double the square footage that way, in one

fell swoop, Violet knew. "So will a little brother or sister for Ava."

Hearing her name, Ava climbed out of the sandbox and toddled back their way. This time she lifted her arms toward Violet. "Up!" she said.

Violet swung their little girl up into her arms and Gavin joined in the family hug. Together, they reflected on how wonderful life was.

* * * * *

Watch for the next story in
Cathy Gillen Thacker's McCABE MULTIPLES
miniseries
LONE STAR TWINS
coming November 2015
Only from Harlequin American Romance!

Staten

WHEN HER OLD hall clock chimed eleven times, Staten Kirkland left Quinn O'Grady's bed. While she slept, he dressed in the shadows, watching her with only the light of the full moon. She'd given him what he needed tonight, and, as always, he felt as if he'd given her nothing.

Walking out to her porch, he studied the newly washed earth, thinking of how empty his life was except for these few hours he shared with Quinn. He'd never love her or anyone, but he wished he could do something for her. Thanks to hard work and inherited land, he was a rich man. She was making a go of her farm, but barely. He could help her if she'd let him. But he knew she'd never let him.

As he pulled on his boots, he thought of a dozen things he could do around the place. Like fixing that old tractor out in the mud or modernizing her irrigation system. The tractor had been sitting out by the road for months. If she'd accept his help, it wouldn't take him an hour to pull the old John Deere out and get the engine running again.

Only, she wouldn't accept anything from him. He knew better than to ask.

He wasn't even sure they were friends some days. Maybe they were more. Maybe less. He looked down at his palm, remembering how she'd rubbed cream on it and worried that all they had in common was loss and the need, now and then, to touch another human being.

The screen door creaked. He turned as Quinn, wrapped in an old quilt, moved out into the night.

"I didn't mean to wake you," he said as she tiptoed across the snow-dusted porch. "I need to get back. Got eighty new yearlings coming in early." He never apologized for leaving, and he wasn't now. He was simply stating facts. With the cattle rustling going on and his plan to enlarge his herd, he might have to hire more men. As always, he felt as though he needed to be on his land and on alert.

She nodded and moved to stand in front of him.

Staten waited. They never touched after they made love. He usually left without a word, but tonight she obviously had something she wanted to say.

Another thing he probably did wrong, he thought. He never complimented her, never kissed her on the mouth, never said any words after he touched her. If she didn't make little sounds of pleasure now and then, he wouldn't have been sure he satisfied her.

Now, standing so close to her, he felt more a stranger than a lover. He knew the smell of her skin, but he had no idea what she was thinking most of the time. She knew quilting and how to make soap from her lavender. She played the piano like an angel and didn't even own a TV. He knew ranching and watched from his recliner every game the Dallas Cowboys played.

If they ever spent over an hour talking they'd probably figure out they had nothing in common. He'd played every sport in high school, and she'd played in both the orchestra and the band. He'd collected most of his college hours online, and she'd gone all the way to New York to school. But they'd loved the same person. Amalah had been Quinn's best friend and his one love. Only, they rarely talked about how they felt. Not anymore. Not ever really. It was too painful, he guessed, for both of them.

Tonight the air was so still, moisture hung like invisible lace. She looked to be closer to her twenties than her forties. Quinn had her own quiet kind of beauty. She always had, and he guessed she still would even when she was old.

To his surprise, she leaned in and kissed his mouth.

He watched her. "You want more?" he finally asked, figuring it was probably the dumbest thing to say to a naked woman standing two inches away from him. He had no idea what *more* would be. They always had sex once, if they had it at all, when he knocked on her door. Sometimes neither made the first move, and they just cuddled on the couch and held each other. Quinn wasn't a passionate woman. What they did was just satisfying a need that they both had now and then.

She kissed him again without saying a word. When her cheek brushed against his stubbled chin, it was wet and tasted newborn like the rain.

Slowly, Staten moved his hands under her blanket and circled her warm body, then he pulled her closer and kissed her fully like he hadn't kissed a woman since his wife died.

Her lips were soft and inviting. When he opened her mouth and invaded, it felt far more intimate than anything they had ever done, but he didn't stop. She wanted this from him, and he had no intention of denying her. No one would ever know that she was the thread that kept him together some days.

When he finally broke the kiss, Quinn was out of breath. She pressed her forehead against his jaw and he waited.

"From now on," she whispered so low he felt her words more than heard them, "when you come to see me, I need you to kiss me goodbye before you go. If I'm asleep, wake me. You don't have to say a word, but you have to kiss me."

She'd never asked him for anything. He had no intention of saying no. His hand spread across the small of her back and pulled her hard against him. "I won't forget if that's what you want." He could feel her heart pounding and knew her asking had not come easy.

She nodded. "It's what I want."

He brushed his lips over hers, loving the way she sighed as if wanting more before she pulled away.

"Good night," she said as though rationing pleasure. Stepping inside, she closed the screen door between them.

Raking his hair back, he put on his hat as he watched her fade into the shadows. The need to return was already building in him. "I'll be back Friday night if it's all right. It'll be late, I've got to visit with my grandmother and do her list of chores before I'll be free. If you like, I could bring barbecue for supper?" He felt as if he was rambling, but something needed to be said, and he had no idea what.

"And vegetables," she suggested.

He nodded. She wanted a meal, not just the meat. "I'll have them toss in sweet potato fries and okra."

She held the blanket tight as if he might see her body. She didn't meet his eyes when he added, "I enjoyed kissing you, Quinn. I look forward to doing so again."

With her head down, she nodded as she vanished into the darkness without a word.

He walked off the porch, deciding if he lived to be a hundred he'd never understand Quinn. As far as he knew, she'd never had a boyfriend when they were in school. And his wife had never told him about Quinn dating anyone special when she went to New York to that fancy music school. Now, in her forties, she'd never had a date, much less a lover that he knew of. But she hadn't been a virgin when they'd made love the first time.

Asking her about her love life seemed far too personal a question.

Climbing into his truck, he forced his thoughts toward problems at the ranch. He needed to hire men; they'd lost three cattle to rustlers this month. As he planned the coming day, Staten did what he always did: he pushed Quinn to a corner of his mind, where she'd wait until he saw her again.

As he passed through the little town of Crossroads, all the businesses were closed up tight except for a gas station that stayed open twenty-four hours to handle the few travelers needing to refuel or brave enough to sample their food.

Half a block away from the station was his grandmother's bungalow, dark amid the cluster of senior citizens' homes. One huge light in the middle of all the little homes shone a low glow on to the porch of each house. The tiny white cottages reminded him of a circle of wagons camped just off the main road. She'd lived fifty years on Kirkland land, but when Staten's granddad, her husband, had died, she'd wanted to move to town. She'd been a teacher in her early years and said she needed to be with her friends in the retirement community, not alone in the big house on the ranch.

He swore without anger, remembering all her instructions the day she moved to town. She wanted her only grandson to drop by every week to switch out batteries, screw in lightbulbs and reprogram the TV that she'd spent the week messing up. He didn't mind dropping by. Besides his father, who considered his home—when he wasn't in Washington—to be Dallas, Granny was the only family Staten had.

A quarter mile past the one main street of Crossroads, his truck lights flashed across four teenagers walking along the road between the Catholic church and the gas station.

Three boys and a girl. Fifteen or sixteen, Staten guessed.

For a moment the memory of Randall came to mind. He'd been about their age when he'd crashed, and he'd worn the same type of blue-and-white letter jacket that two of the boys wore tonight.

Staten slowed as he passed them. "You kids need a ride?" The lights were still on at the church, and a few cars were in the parking lot. Saturday night, Staten remembered. Members of 4-H would probably be working in the basement on projects.

One kid waved. A tall Hispanic boy named Lucas, whom he thought was the oldest son of the head wrangler on the Collins Ranch. Reyes was his last name, and Staten remembered the boy being one of a dozen young kids who were often hired part-time at the ranch.

Staten had heard the kid was almost as good a wrangler as his father. The magic of working with horses must have been passed down from father to son, along with the height. Young Reyes might be lean but, thanks to working, he would be in better shape than either of the football boys. When Lucas Reyes finished high school, he'd have no trouble hiring on at any of the big ranches, including the Double K.

"No, we're fine, Mr. Kirkland," the Reyes boy said politely. "We're just walking down to the station for a Coke. Reid Collins's brother is picking us up soon."

"No crime in that, mister," a redheaded kid in a letter jacket answered. His words came fast and clipped, reminding Staten of how his son had sounded.

Volume from a boy trying to prove he was a man, Staten thought.

He couldn't see the faces of the two boys with letter jackets, but the girl kept her head up. "We've been working on a project for the fair," she answered politely. "I'm Lauren Brigman, Mr. Kirkland."

Staten nodded. *Sheriff Brigman's daughter, I remember you.* She knew enough to be polite, but it was none of his business. "Good evening, Lauren," he said. "Nice to see you again. Good luck with the project."

When he pulled away, he shook his head. Normally, he wouldn't have bothered to stop. This might be small-town Texas, but they were not his problem. If he saw the Reyes boy again, he would apologize.

Staten swore. At this rate he'd turn into a nosy old man by forty-five. It didn't seem that long ago that he and Amalah used to walk up to the gas station after meetings at the church.

Hell, maybe Quinn asking to kiss him had rattled him more than he thought. He needed to get his head straight. She was just a friend. A woman he turned to when the storms came. Nothing more. That was the way they both wanted it.

Until he made it back to her porch next Friday night, he had a truckload of trouble at the ranch to worry about.

Lauren

A MIDNIGHT MOON blinked its way between storm clouds as Lauren Brigman cleaned the mud off her shoes. The guys had gone inside the gas station for Cokes. She didn't really want anything to drink, but it was either walk over with the others after working on their fair projects or stay back at the church and talk to Mrs. Patterson.

Somewhere Mrs. Patterson had gotten the idea that since Lauren didn't have a mother around, she should take every opportunity to have a "girl talk" with the sheriff's daughter.

Lauren wanted to tell the old woman that she had known all the facts of life by the age of seven, and she really did not need a buddy to share her teenage years with. Besides, her mother lived in Dallas. It wasn't like she'd died. She'd just left. Just because she couldn't stand the sight of Lauren's dad didn't mean she didn't call and talk to Lauren almost every week. Maybe Mom had just gotten tired of the sheriff's nightly lectures. Lauren had heard every one of Pop's talks so many times that she had them memorized in alphabetical order.

Her grades put her at the top of the sophomore class, and she saw herself bound for college in less than three years. Lauren had no intention of getting pregnant, or doing drugs, or any of the other fearful situations Mrs. Patterson and her father had hinted might befall her. Her pop didn't even want her dating until she was sixteen, and, judging from the boys she knew in high school, she'd just as soon go dateless until eighteen. Maybe college would have better pickings. Some of these guys were so dumb she was surprised they got their cowboy hats on straight every morning.

Reid Collins walked out from the gas station first with a can of Coke in each hand. "I bought you one even though you said you didn't want anything to drink," he announced as he neared. "Want to lean on me while you clean your shoes?"

Lauren rolled her eyes. Since he'd grown a few inches and started working out, Reid thought he was God's gift to girls.

"Why?" she asked as she tossed the stick. "I have a brick wall to lean on. And don't get any ideas we're on a date, Reid, just because I walked over here with you."

"I don't date sophomores," he snapped. "I'm on first string, you know. I could probably date any senior I want to. Besides, you're like a little sister, Lauren. We've known each other since you were in the first grade."

She thought of mentioning that playing first string on a football team that only had forty players total, including the coaches and water boy, wasn't any great accomplishment, but arguing with Reid would rot her brain. He'd been born rich, and he'd thought he knew everything since he cleared the birth canal. She feared his disease was terminal.

"If you're cold, I'll let you wear my football jacket." When she didn't comment, he bragged, "I had to reorder a bigger size after a month of working out."

She hated to, but if she didn't compliment him soon, he'd never stop begging. "You look great in the jacket, Reid. Half the seniors on the team aren't as big as you." There was nothing wrong with Reid from the neck down. In a few years he'd be a knockout with the Collins good looks and trademark rusty hair, not quite brown, not quite red. But he still wouldn't interest her.

"So, when I get my driver's license next month, do you want to take a ride?"

Lauren laughed. "You've been asking that since I was in the third grade and you got your first bike. The answer is still no. We're friends, Reid. We'll always be friends, I'm guessing."

He smiled a smile that looked as if he'd been practicing. "I know, Lauren, but I keep wanting to give you a chance now and then. You know, some guys don't want to date the sheriff's daughter, and I hate to point it out, babe, but if you don't fill out some, it's going to be bad news in college." He had the nerve to point at her chest.

"I know." She managed to pull off a sad look. "Having my father is a cross I have to bear. Half the guys in town are afraid of him. Like he might arrest them for talking to me. Which he might." She had no intention of discussing her lack of curves with Reid.

"No, it's not fear of him, exactly," Reid corrected. "I think it's more the bullet holes they're afraid of. Every time a guy looks at you, your old man starts patting his service weapon. Nerve-racking habit, if you ask me. From the looks of it, I seem to be the only one he'll let stand beside you, and that's just because our dads are friends."

She grinned. Reid was spoiled and conceited and self-centered, but he was right. They'd probably always be friends. Her dad was the sheriff, and his was the mayor of Crossroads, even though he lived five miles from town on one of the first ranches established near Ransom Canyon.

With her luck, Reid would be the only guy in the state that her father would let her date. Grumpy old Pop had what she called Terminal Cop Disease. Her father thought everyone, except his few friends, was most likely a criminal, anyone under thirty should be stopped and searched, and anyone who'd ever smoked pot could not be trusted.

Tim O'Grady, Reid's eternal shadow, walked out of the station with a huge frozen drink. The clear cup showed off its red-and-yellow layers of cherry-and-pineapple-flavored sugar.

Where Reid was balanced in his build, Tim was lanky, disjointed. He seemed to be made of mismatched parts. His arms were too long. His feet seemed too big, and his wired smile barely fit in his mouth. When he took a deep draw on his drink, he staggered and held his forehead from the brain freeze.

Lauren laughed as he danced around like a puppet with his strings crossed. Timothy, as the teachers called him, was always good for a laugh. He had the depth of cheap paint but the imagination of a natural-born storyteller.

"Maybe I shouldn't have gotten an icy drink on such a cold night," he mumbled between gulps. "If I freeze from the inside out, put me up on Main Street as a statue."

Lauren giggled.

Lucas Reyes was the last of their small group to come outside. Lucas hadn't bought anything, but he evidently was avoiding standing outside with her. She'd known Lucas Reyes for a few years, maybe longer, but he never talked to her. Like Reid and Tim, he was a year ahead of her, but since he rarely talked, she usually only noticed him as a background person in her world.

Unlike them, Lucas didn't have a family name following him around opening doors for a hundred miles.

They all four lived east of Crossroads along the rambling canyon called Ransom Canyon. Lauren and her father lived in one of a cluster of houses near the lake, as did Tim's parents. Reid's family ranch was five miles farther out. She had no idea where Lucas's family lived. Maybe on the Collins Ranch. His father worked on the Bar W, which had been in the Collins family for over a hundred years. The area around the headquarters looked like a small village.

Reid repeated the plan. "My brother said he'd drop Sharon off and be back for us. But if they get busy doing their thing it could be an hour. We might as well walk back and sit on the church steps."

"Great fun," Tim complained. "Everything's closed. It's freezing out here, and I swear this town is so dead somebody should bury it."

"We could start walking toward home," Lauren suggested as she pulled a tiny flashlight from her key chain. The canyon lake wasn't more than a mile. If they walked they wouldn't be so cold. She could probably be home before Reid's dumb brother could get his lips off Sharon. If rumors were true, Sharon had very kissable lips, among other body parts.

"Better than standing around here," Reid said as Tim kicked mud toward the building. "I'd rather be walking than sitting. Plus, if we go back to the church, Mrs. Patterson will probably come out to keep us company."

Without a vote, they started walking. Lauren didn't like the idea of stumbling into mud holes now covered up by a dusting of snow along the side of the road, but it sounded better than standing out front of the gas station. Besides, the moon offered enough light, making the tiny flashlight her father insisted she carry worthless.

Within a few yards, Reid and Tim had fallen behind and were lighting up a smoke. To her surprise, Lucas stayed beside her.

"You don't smoke?" she asked, not really expecting him to answer.

"No, can't afford the habit," he said, surprising her. "I've got plans, and they don't include lung cancer."

Maybe the dark night made it easier to talk, or maybe Lauren didn't want to feel so alone in the shadows. "I was starting to think you were a mute. We've had a few classes together, and you've never said a word. Even tonight you were the only one who didn't talk about your project."

Lucas shrugged. "Didn't see the point. I'm just entering for the prize money, not trying to save the world or build a better tomorrow."

She giggled.

He laughed, too, realizing he'd just made fun of the whole point of the projects. "Plus," he added, "there's just not much opportunity to get a word in around those two." He nodded his head at the two letter jackets falling farther behind as a cloud of smoke haloed above them.

She saw his point. The pair trailed them by maybe twenty feet or more, and both were talking about football. Neither seemed to require a listener.

"Why do you hang out with them?" she asked. Lucas didn't seem to fit. Studious and quiet, he hadn't gone out for sports or joined many clubs that she knew about. "Jocks usually hang out together."

"I wanted to work on my project tonight, and Reid offered me a ride. Listening to football talk beats walking in this weather."

Lauren tripped into a pothole. Lucas's hand shot out and caught her in the darkness. He steadied her, then let go.

"Thanks. You saved my life," she joked.

"Hardly, but if I had, you'd owe me a blood debt."

"Would I have to pay?"

"Of course. It would be a point of honor. You'd have to save me or be doomed to a coward's hell."

"Lucky you just kept me from tripping, or I'd be following you around for years waiting to repay the debt." She rubbed her arm where he'd touched her. He was stronger than she'd thought he would be. "You lift weights?"

The soft laughter came again. "Yeah, it's called work. Until I was sixteen, I spent the summers and every weekend working on Reid's father's ranch. Once I was old enough, I signed up at the Kirkland place to cowboy when they need extras. Every dime I make is going to college tuition in a year. That's why I don't have a car yet. When I get to college, I won't need it, and the money will go toward books."

"But you're just a junior. You've still got a year and a half of high school."

"I've got it worked out so I can graduate early. High school's a waste of time. I've got plans. I can make a hundred-fifty a day working, and my dad says he thinks I'll be able to cowboy every day I'm not in school this spring and all summer."

She tripped again, and his hand steadied her once more. Maybe it was her imagination, but she swore he held on a little longer than necessary.

"You're an interesting guy, Lucas Reyes."

"I will be," he said. "Once I'm in college, I can still come home and work breaks and weekends. I'm thinking I can take a few online classes during the summer, live at home and save enough to pay for the next year. I'm going to Tech no matter what it takes."

"You planning on getting through college in three years, too?"

He shook his head. "Don't know if I can. But I'll have the degree, whatever it is, before I'm twenty-two."

No one her age had ever talked of the future like that. Like they were just passing through this time in their life and something yet to come mattered far more. "When you are somebody, I think I'd like to be your friend."

"I hope we will be more than that, Lauren." His words were so low, she wasn't sure she heard them.

"Hey, you two deadbeats up there!" Reid yelled. "I got an idea."

Lauren didn't want the conversation with Lucas to end, but if she ignored Reid he'd just get louder. "What?"

Reid ran up between them and put an arm over both her and Lucas's shoulders. "How about we break into the Gypsy House? I hear it's haunted by Gypsies who died a hundred years ago."

Tim caught up to them. As always, he agreed with Reid. "Look over there in the trees. The place is just waiting for us. Heard if you rattle a Gypsy's bones, the dead will speak to you." Tim's eyes glowed in the moonlight. "I had a cousin once who said he heard voices in that old place, and no one was there but him."

"This is not a good idea." Lauren tried to back away, but Reid held her shoulder tight.

"Come on, Lauren, for once in your life, do something that's not safe. No one's lived in the old place for years. How much trouble can we get into?"

Tim's imagination had gone wild. According to him all kinds of things could happen. They might find a body. Ghosts could run them out, or the spirit of a Gypsy might take over their minds. Who knew, zombies might sleep in the rubble of old houses.

Lauren rolled her eyes. She didn't want to think of the zombies getting Tim. A walking dead with braces was too much.

"It's just a rotting old house," Lucas said so low no one heard but Lauren. "There's probably rats or rotten floors. It's an accident waiting to happen. How about you come back in the daylight, Reid, if you really want to explore the place?"

"We're all going, now," Reid announced, as he shoved Lauren off the road and into the trees that blocked the view of the old homestead from passing cars. "Think of the story we'll have to tell everyone Monday. We will have explored a haunted house and lived to tell the tale."

Reason told her to protest more strongly, but at fifteen, reason wasn't as intense as the possibility of an adventure. Just once, she'd have a story to tell. Just this once…her father wouldn't find out.

They rattled across the rotting porch steps fighting tumbleweeds that stood like flimsy guards around the place. The door was locked and boarded up. The smell of decay hung in the foggy air, and a tree branch scraped against one side of the house as if whispering for them to stay back.

The old place didn't look like much. It might have been the remains of an early settlement, built solid to face the winters with no style or charm. Odds were, Gypsies never even lived in it. It appeared to be a half dugout with a second floor built on years later. The first floor was planted down into the earth a few feet, so the second-floor windows were just above their heads, giving the place the look of a house that had been stepped on by a giant.

Everyone called it the Gypsy House because a group of hippies had squatted there in the seventies. They'd painted a peace sign on one wall, but it had faded and been rained on until it almost looked like a witching sign. No one remembered when the hippies had moved on or who owned the house now, but somewhere in its past a family named

Stanley must have lived there because old-timers called it the Stanley house.

"I heard devil worshippers lived here years ago." Tim began making scary-movie-soundtrack noises. "Body parts are probably scattered in the basement. They say once Satan moves in, only the blood of a virgin will wash the place clean."

Reid's laughter sounded nervous. "That leaves me out."

Tim jabbed his friend. "You wish. I say you'll be the first to scream when a dead hand, not connected to a body, touches you."

"Shut up, Tim." Reid's uneasy voice echoed in the night. "You're freaking me out. Besides, there is no basement. It's just a half dugout built into the ground, so we'll find no buried bodies."

Lauren screamed as Reid kicked a low window in, and all the guys laughed.

"You go first, Lucas," Reid ordered. "I'll stand guard."

To Lauren's surprise, Lucas slipped into the space. His feet hit the ground with a thud somewhere in the blackness.

"You next, Tim," Reid announced as if he were the commander.

"Nope. I'll go after you." All Tim's laughter had disappeared. Apparently he'd frightened himself.

"I'll go." Lauren suddenly wanted this entire adventure to be over with. With her luck, animals were wintering in the old place.

"I'll help you down." Reid lowered her into the window space.

As she moved through total darkness, her feet wouldn't quite touch the bottom. For a moment she just hung, afraid to tell Reid to drop her.

Then she felt Lucas's hands at her waist. Slowly he took her weight.

"I'm in," she called back to Reid. He let her hands go, and she dropped against Lucas.

"You all right?" Lucas whispered near her hair.

"This was a dumb idea."

She felt him laugh more than she heard it. "That you talking or the Gypsy's advice? Of all the brains dropping in here tonight, yours would probably be the most interesting to take over, so watch out. A ghost might just climb in your head and let free all the secret thoughts you keep inside, Lauren."

He pulled her a foot into the blackness as a letter jacket dropped through the window. His hands circled her waist. She could feel him breathing as Reid finally landed, cussing the darkness. For a moment it seemed all right for Lucas to stay close; then in a blink, he was gone from her side.

Now the tiny flashlight offered Lauren some much-needed light. The house was empty except for an old wire bed frame and a few broken stools. With Reid in the lead, they moved up rickety stairs to the second floor, where shadowy light came from big dirty windows.

Tim hesitated when the floor's boards began to rock as if the entire second story were on some kind of seesaw. He backed down the steps a few feet, letting the others go first. "I don't know if this second story will hold us all." Fear rattled in his voice.

Reid laughed and teased Tim as he stomped across the second floor, making the entire room buck and pitch. "Come on up, Tim. This place is better than a fun house."

Stepping hesitantly on the upstairs floor, Lauren felt Lucas just behind her and knew he was watching over her.

Tim dropped down a few more steps, not wanting to even try.

Lucas backed against the wall between the windows, his hand still brushing Lauren's waist to keep her steady as Reid jumped to make the floor shake. The whole house seemed to moan in pain, like a hundred-year-old man standing up one arthritic joint at a time.

When Reid yelled for Tim to join them, Tim started back up the broken stairs, just before the second floor buckled and crumbled. Tim dropped out of sight as rotten lumber pinned him halfway between floors.

His scream of pain ended Reid's laughter.

In a blink, dust and boards flew as pieces of the roof rained down on them and the second floor vanished below them, board by rotting board.

She'd know that butt anywhere. Hunter Boone.

In eleven years, his derriere hadn't changed much. And, apparently, the view still managed to take her breath away.

"Need some help with that, Josie?" Her father's voice made her wince.

She was clutching a tray of her dad's famous German breakfast kolaches and hiding behind the display counter. Why was she—a rational, professional woman—ducking behind a bakery counter? Because *he'd* walked in.

She shot her father a look as she said, "Thanks, Dad. I've got it." Taking a deep breath, she stood slowly and slid the tray into the display cabinet with care.

"Josie? Josie Stephens?" a high-pitched voice asked. "Oh my God, look at you. Why, you haven't changed since high school."

Josie glanced at the woman but couldn't place her, so she smiled and said, "Thanks. You, too."

That was when her gaze wandered to Hunter. He was waiting. And, from the look on his face, he *knew* Josie had no idea who the woman was.

"So it's true?" the woman continued. "Your dad said you were coming to help him, but I couldn't imagine you back *here*. We *all* know how much you hated Stonewall Crossing." Josie remembered her then. Winnie Michaels. "What did you call it, redneck hell—right?" Winnie kept going, teasing—but with a definite edge. "Guess hell froze over."

"Kind of hard to say no when your dad needs you," Josie answered, forcing herself not to snap.

Her father jumped to her defense. "She wasn't about to let her old man try to run this place on his own."

"It's kinda weird to see the two of you standing here." Winnie glanced back and forth between Josie and Hunter. "I mean, without having your tongues down each other's throats and all."

Hunter wasn't smiling anymore. "I've gotta get these to the boys."

Josie saw him take the huge box by the register. A swift kick of disappointment prompted her to blurt out, "Too bad, Hunter. If I remember it correctly, you knew how to kiss a girl."

"If you remember? Ouch." His eyes swept her face, lingering on her lips. "Have fun while you're back in hell, Jo. I'll see you around."

Don't miss
A COWBOY'S CHRISTMAS REUNION
by Sasha Summers,
available in October 2015 wherever
Harlequin® American Romance®
books and ebooks are sold.

www.Harlequin.com